MURDER
AT
MORGAN
HOUSE

Janet Winters

To Sally —
my wonderful
friend —
keep the smiles
regards coming!
XOXO
Janet

Janet Winters
P.O. Box 86
Ligonier, PA 15658

Publisher's Note: This is a work of fiction. Names, characters, places, and incidents are a product of the author's imagination. Locales and public names are sometimes used for atmospheric purposes. Any resemblance to actual people, living or dead, or to businesses, companies, events, institutions, or locales is completely coincidental.

Murder at Morgan House/ Janet Winters. -- 1st ed.

CHAPTER ONE

I had the perfect opportunity to murder Bart. I had the motive, too.

Only a consummate narcissist like Bart Skeleton, Esq., would have the audacity to marry two women in the same place at the same time and think he could get away with it. It was bad enough that he screwed me over, but his own children! We had *twins* when he married Marion Fallon. What did he think would become of them? But then again, we have to remember that Bart never did think of anyone but himself.

Dr. Templeton Frick picked up his pad and pencil and started taking notes. "How did Bart's behavior make you feel, Ivy?

"How did it make me feel? Devastated, humiliated, heartbroken , Doctor, that's how it made me feel. I spent countless hours trying to figure out where I went wrong. Was I such a terrible wife that he felt like he needed another one to compensate for me? And as far as my own judgment goes—what was I thinking when I married him in the first place?"

"Have you worked through any of these feelings, Ivy?"

"No, I don't think I have worked through them, Doctor. That's why I'm in therapy."

I hope this guy knows what he's doing. If not, it serves me right for picking a therapist out of the Yellow Pages. He does have an assortment of framed diplomas all over the walls, so that's a little reassuring anyway.

I suppose some people might think Bart was justified in his self-admiration. After all, he was a very successful criminal defense attorney, whose specialty was rape and murder. He was very much in demand. He was certainly good-looking in a suave Michael Douglas sort of way, and he had managed to ingratiate himself with the upper echelons of Philadelphia society, garnering invitations to all the best parties. Bart was the golden boy.

"I felt plenty sorry for myself, Doctor, but strangely enough I felt sorry for Marion, too. I mean, I did resent her, of course, but after all Bart duped her too. After I met her, I realized that she deserved justice almost as much as I did. Although jail would be too good for him, after weighing the pros and cons I realized that in the unlikely event that I would be convicted, it wasn't worth life in prison, or heaven forbid, the electric chair to get even with Bart. But get even with him I did."

Dr. Frick squirmed slightly in his giant leather chair. He removed his rimless glasses and smoothed back his thinning silver hair. He pulled down the sleeves of his brown tweed jacket, and struggled to launch himself into a standing position. "I'm sorry Ivy, but that's all the time we have for today. We'll have to explore your feelings about Bart in more detail next week. I'll see you then, same time," he said with a half-hearted smile.

I took the ancient elevator to the lobby and stepped out onto the sidewalk, taking in a deep breath of fresh spring air. I could smell the sweet fragrance of the daffodils that were popping up in everyone's front yard; I took a moment to enjoy this fleeting time, when nature comes to life. There was a soft breeze blowing and it ruffled my long blonde hair; I should have worn a hat.

Walking back to the parking lot a small sign caught my eye. It was planted in the front yard of an impressive Victorian-style home, and said *Historic Morgan House circa 1837.* I love architecture and design, and I get excited when I stumble across a great example of period style. I was studying the lines when I noticed the figure of a man in the window. He appeared to be an older guy from what I could tell. He was dressed in plaid, which did nothing for his physique, but the red bow tie he wore was an interesting accent—don't see many of those nowadays. Our eyes met, and I was a little embarrassed to be caught staring at his house. I gave him a friendly wave, but he just stood there, perfectly still, and did not wave back. A creepy feeling came over me and I quickly moved on.

As I passed by the Coach House B&B next door, I saw Roberta Bristol cleaning the turquoise green gingerbread trim on her porch banisters. "Good morning, Roberta. Beautiful day, isn't it?" I said.

She looked up from her task, and squinted at me. "Ivy Snow? Is that you?" Roberta never wanted to wear her glasses. She thought they made her look old. Well, she was sixty-five if she was a day.

"Yes, Roberta," I said with a sigh.

She pulled down her navy blue Nittany Lion sweatshirt in an effort to conceal the ten pounds she had gained over the holidays. The extra weight didn't do her any favors. She was short to begin with, probably about five feet, five feet one at best. She wore her black kinky hair piled high on top of her head in an effort to add inches, but the effect was more like an afro that had seen better days.

"Looks like we're finally getting a spring," she said with a toothy smile.

It was especially good news for her; warmer spring weather would bring back the tourists.

"Hey, Roberta, I just passed by Morgan House and I saw a guy standing in the window. Who is he?"

"He's a pain in the butt, that's who he is. Name's Mike Smythe. Michael Tellington Smythe, to be precise," she said with an air of haughtiness meant to characterize him.

I looked at her quizzically, egging her to go on.

I can't stand that guy. He thinks he knows everything. He says I have no taste. Can you imagine that?"

"What do you mean?" I asked.

"He had the nerve to go to the zoning board and file a complaint about the color I painted my B&B. Said it was garish, and that I was ruining the understated beauty of East Main Street. He is insisting that I repaint the house in a more subtle color to blend in with the other buildings. White bread and mayonnaise, if you ask me."

"Really?" I said, trying my best to sound indignant just to get into the spirit of things.

"I'm not about to spend another $8,000 to have this place repainted. Besides, my guests love the color. I've heard more than one person comment that Candy Apple Red makes them feel warm and welcome." She shook her finger. "Little does that troublemaker know I happen to be on the zoning board of this town, and his petition is going straight into the circular file, where it belongs."

"You show 'em, Roberta," I said, and went on my way, making a mental note to stay on her good side.

I hopped into my little BMW Roadster and spun around Wellington Towne Commons on my way to a meeting at the Field & Stream Club. The landscape crews were hard at work mulching and fertilizing to create the stunning gardens that were the pride and joy of the citizens of Wellington, Pennsylvania.

I moved to Wellington, well, actually I moved to a small horse farm just outside of town, right after Bart was incarcerated. He got five years on the bigamy charge, and I can still hear his parting words ringing in my ears. "I'll get you for this, you bitch." Of course, Bart blamed me for the fact that he was going to jail. Never mind that he was the one who committed the crime.

I swerved my car to miss Dr. Corbin Montrose, plastic surgeon, dressed in his Revolutionary War garb on the way to re-enact the Battle of Wellington. Wellingtonians are passionate about their historic roots. Every war fought on American soil included at least one battle in Wellington. With all of that cannon fire going on, it's a wonder the town is still standing. Fortunately, my Roadster has good torque, and I was able to avoid smashing into The Folly; a lacy white Victorian structure set in the center of the commons. It is the symbol of Wellington itself, and serves as bandstand, photo op, preteen hangout, and wedding chapel. Many a union has been sealed there by the mayor of Wellington, who also happens to be the town's premier appliance repairman. For all of Wellington's quintessential small-town charm, I couldn't help but sense sinister underpinnings. It's like that old cliché, *if it seems too good to be true, it probably is.* I was about to find out that clichés stand the test of time for a reason.

CHAPTER TWO

Driving slowly up the long lane that led to the Field & Stream Club, I kept a sharp eye out for deer, golf carts, and anything else that might get in my way. I pulled into a parking space in the upper lot and headed for the front door of the clubhouse. Stanley Klink, the short pudgy doorman, was standing just inside, ready to assist members as they entered.

I handed him my Burberry. "Stanley, has Crystal Prichard arrived yet?"

"No, Ms. Snow, you're the first one here," he said.

Crystal is my new friend in Wellington. She's the real estate agent that I worked with while looking for a home in the area. Although she grew up here, she's kind of a misfit: a little bohemian in style, and kind of flighty. People are somewhat wary of her because in her business she finds out where all the bodies are buried. She can be a little gossipy at times; nothing vicious—she just likes having the "scoop." Crystal and I are co-chairs of the annual charity dinner and antiques auction, and we like arranging the details of the event ourselves, leaving nothing to chance.

While waiting around, I stuck my head into the doorway of the Stag Bar, which is located directly across from Stanley's station. I thought I'd see if anyone was doing any daytime drinking. The room was fairly empty, just a few old geezers hanging around. I quickly spotted the fellow that I had seen earlier in the day standing at the window of the Morgan House. Mike Smythe, that's what Roberta told me his name was. He was belly up to the bar nursing a Scotch neat, or maybe it was an Old-Fashioned. The guy sitting next to him must have just told a hilarious joke, because suddenly Smythe threw his head back with laughter. Although the lighting was dim, I had a much better view of him than I did through the front window of Morgan House.

Mr. Smythe was dressed in a beige and brown tattersall-checked shirt topped with a camel corduroy blazer. He was wearing horn-rimmed glasses, and the same red bow tie that he had on earlier. He finished off the ensemble with khaki trousers and brown Docksiders. The preppy, old money look that typified the club. There was something about him, though, that piqued my curiosity. I would've walked in and introduced myself, but much to our chagrin women are not allowed in the Stag Bar at the Field & Stream Club. Jacket and penis required.

"Stanley, do you know that guy with the red bow tie?

"Sure, that's Mr. Smythe."

"Is he a member here?

"Yes," said Stanley. "He's retired now, but he used to be a big shot in the newspaper business in Philadelphia."

"Really? Which paper?"

"It was the Philadelphia Press. He was second in command, next to Mr. Hess."

"Do you know how long ago that was?"

"No, I really don't know that much about him," Stanley said as he hung up my coat.

The Philadelphia Press...I thought back to the people I might have known there over the years, and then it dawned on me. Mike Smythe had been president of the Press when I worked as public relations director for *Horse & Hound* magazine. I remember going to a luncheon at the News Club where he was guest speaker. He looked quite different back then. He had more hair, he was trimmer and, if I recall correctly, his face was chiseled rather than puffy, as it is now. What do I remember about Mike Smythe? I think my only dialogue with him was "how do you do?" when we were introduced. There was something about the man that seemed, well, phony. In part, I think it was the talk he gave that day. The topic had something to do with the supposedly symbiotic relationship between his editors and the PR people that dogged them. I don't know why, but after all of his rhetoric about fostering good relationships, I had the distinct feeling that if I had called his office an hour later I would *not* have been put through.

But there was something else. I racked my brain. And then it all started to come back to me. Michael Smythe was the last client that Bart represented before going up on bigamy charges. He came home from the office one day all smug and pleased with himself for landing a high-profile embezzlement case. He said that there was some big dustup at the Philadelphia Press over money that was missing from the till, and that the owner, Victor Hess, was blaming the president, Michael Smythe.

His client, the defendant in this case, was Michael Tellington Smythe, former president and managing director of the Philadelphia Press. The Press is the region's largest and oldest news outlet. They claim to be an offshoot of Ben Franklin's *Poor Richard's Almanac*. The paper was currently owned by Victor Brownfield Hess, a Pittsburgh native whose name appeared on Forbes list of the top 100 richest people in America.

Hess had hired his old buddy, Michael Tellington Smythe, to oversee the running of his newspaper.

As the heir to a Pittsburgh steel fortune, Smythe was no piker in the money department himself. He and Hess went way back to their boyhood days at Sewickley Academy, and traveled in the same social circles all of their lives. Although Smythe preferred to live in the

Pittsburgh area, where he had political influence, he moved to Philadelphia to run the Press.

Hess's primary purpose for owning the Press, among other media holdings, was power. Hess believed that if you controlled the media you controlled the country, and on that score he was probably right.

Victor Hess, who was the plaintiff in the case, was an interesting character. Born and raised in Pittsburgh, he was the only child produced by the marriage of banking and railroads. His mother and father were both financial royalty, and they sought to instill in their son a sense of civic duty—perhaps even serving in the highest office in the land. The civic interest was instilled, but not in the way they expected.

Victor was intensely interested in politics, but he had no interest in running for office. He figured out, quite early on, that to control public opinion was the real power, so he set off to make sure that his viewpoints were adopted by those voters who would determine which politicians got elected and which didn't. His values were intensely conservative, and worked out well with the mindset of the rural Pennsylvania constituency known for holding onto their guns and religion. Victor's problem was with the liberal Democratic machine that was in bed with the unions.

To address that issue, Victor chose to marry Sheila Federici, daughter of Joseph L. Federici, president of the

United Steelworkers union. Sheila was an unabashed social climber who was raised having the best that money could buy. But there was one thing that money couldn't buy, and that was social status. Invitations to all the right parties, seats on all the right charitable boards, and memberships in the most exclusive clubs. For those, one needed another kind of currency. Currency provided by the name Hess. So, it was a marriage made in heaven, except for one thing—Victor and Sheila hated each other with a passion.

The big trouble at the Philadelphia Press had been some time in the making. Victor Hess was sitting behind his huge mahogany desk in the chief executive offices. He was feeling out of sorts that morning. He'd had another fight with Shelia the night before that ended with the threat of divorce. To add to his headache, he had a meeting scheduled with Mike Smythe to discuss the paper's declining revenues. Just as he finished his second cup of coffee, Smythe knocked on his door. "Come in, Michael. Have a seat." Victor's irritability was apparent.

Mike knew that this meeting would not be a pleasant one and had been dreading it for days.

Victor dove right in. "Mike, we both know why we're here. The revenues for the Press have been in a downward spiral for the past two months."

Mike swallowed hard. "I told Dave Sutter, that idiot sales manager, to get those lazy account executives off their asses." When under the gun, Mike's first tactic was to always place the blame squarely on someone else's shoulders.

"I don't know if the staff is completely at fault," said Hess.

"No, you are right." Mike's second tactic was to always agree with the boss. "What we need are better incentives for the advertisers. The big department stores are struggling in this recession, so orders are down and ad sizes have been shrinking."

"Have you had drinks with Wanamaker lately?" Victor firmly believed that the old boy network could always be relied upon.

"Well, not lately," Mike sputtered. He knew that drinks with Wanamaker, Philadelphia's biggest department store mogul, wouldn't get him out of the mess he was in.

"Perhaps it's time you do that."

"Sure, Victor, I'll call him this afternoon."

Hess sat back in his chair and folded his arms across his chest. "Mike, I don't care what it takes. You need to get the situation under control immediately—we are hemorrhaging money."

"Yes, yes, I understand. I'll go over the numbers again and get back to you with a solid plan by the end of the week." Mike looked at his watch and realized he was running late. "Victor, I have to go. I am guest speaker at the News Club luncheon today."

"Remember, by the end of the week, Mike," Victor stated with emphasis.

Mike couldn't get out of there fast enough. He had been in some tight spots before, but never anything like this. In all fairness, he had no choice in doing what he'd done. He had run into some bad luck at the track, well some really bad luck...but it happens to everyone. He'd had to pay those bookies or God knows what they would have done to him. He'd had to get the money somewhere, so he borrowed it from the Press account. He would have put it back by now if that losing streak hadn't been so relentless. So far, he had been able to juggle the books to hide some of the losses, but that tactic was no longer viable. He had to find a way out of this, and fast. One thing for sure, he certainly wasn't going to find it at the News Club. Those people were just a bunch of losers hanging around having a bitch-fest about their crappy jobs, and their crappy lives in general. He'd make his speech quickly—they'd appreciate that—and then figure out what to do.

Mike was right on all counts. That audience loved a quick speech; didn't matter what you said, as long as you got it over with fast. And, there was the usual roundup of losers in attendance. He was glad-handing his way to the door when the public relations director from his own paper approached him with an attractive woman in tow. "Mike Smythe, I'd like you to meet Ivy Snow Skeleton." Mike said his perfunctory how-do-you-do's, then something stopped him in his tracks. That woman's name, Ivy Snow *Skeleton.* He recognized that name. He racked his brain trying to remember. Of course, Bartholomew Skeleton, the highly acclaimed criminal defense lawyer. That was the answer to his dilemma. He needed a man like Bart Skeleton in his corner.

Bart had been really excited because he knew that the other media outlets would jump all over a nice juicy scandal at the competition. That meant that Bart would be all over TV, radio, and the other newspapers. He would go viral on the web. He would become a celebrity lawyer like Johnny Cochran. There would be no stopping him. Fame and fortune would be his. Well, the fame part kinda happened, but not for the reason he expected. Bart's jail sentence for bigamy was hot news for a while.

Victor Hess later dropped the charges against Smythe, for what reason no one knew. Smythe must have moved to Wellington shortly after that.

Crystal finally arrived wearing some sort of blue and yellow gypsy dress with gold sandals and dangly earrings. Not quite appropriate for the Field & Stream Club, but eccentricity was part of her charm. She whispered in my ear, "Have I got a story for you! I'll tell you after the meeting."

My curiosity was piqued, to say the least. Crystal knew everything about everyone in Wellington.

We headed straight for the front desk, and I told the uniformed receptionist standing guard that we were here to meet with the executive chef and the dining room manager about our upcoming event. She instructed us to wait in the Living Room, the most beautiful room in the club.

There was an aura of stillness about the place. One felt compelled to whisper. The wool broadloom carpeting muffled our steps as we entered the room. Portraits in oil, with heavy gilt frames, gazed at us. The bookshelves were lined with leather-bound tomes and bric-a-brac featuring game birds and sporting dogs. Every surface glowed—the dark mahogany wood furniture, the brass hardware on the French doors and windows, the sterling silver tea service on the butler's tray in front of the fireplace. Magnificent fresh flower arrangements were strategically placed around the room, filling the air with a pleasing aroma. It was so me—I could move in any time!

We met with the chef and manager, and agreed on the bourbon roasted pork tenderloin for the entrée, accompanied by fingerling potatoes, baby asparagus spears (which they grow right on the club grounds), and crème brûlée for dessert. I adjourned the meeting and herded Crystal right to the ladies' room.

"Okay, so what's the big scoop?" I was dying to know.

"Victor Hess and his wife are getting a divorce."

"No kidding?" Funny, it was the second time today I'd heard the name Victor Hess.

"You know, he's one of the richest men in the country, and pretty soon he'll be on the market again."

"Crystal—you're not seriously suggesting?"

"Well, I don't know. We'll have to play this one by ear. I heard there's no prenup."

"Ouch!" I said. I gave Crystal a peck on the cheek and left her standing in front of the vanity trying to tame her frizzy auburn mane.

I made my way to the front door of the club, where Stanley was overwhelmed by an onslaught of dowagers arriving for afternoon tea. I started for the parking lot, and just ahead of me sauntered Mike Smythe. He was making his way to a green vintage Cadillac Eldorado, so I slowed my pace to observe him. He reached the driver's-side door and stopped abruptly. He glanced to his left, then his right to see if he was being watched. Satisfied of his solitude, he dropped a cigar butt into the lush daffodil bed and grounded it into the earth, crushing delicate yellow petals under the heel of his Docksiders.

CHAPTER THREE

On my way home from the Field & Stream Club I stopped by the school to pick up my son, Jayson. Handsome Jayson, with the shaggy blond hair and piercing blue eyes, was the masculine version of his twin sister, Jaycee. He had just finished with baseball practice and dumped his backpack and equipment in the trunk.

He hopped into the car and handed me a note printed on official school stationary. I opened it—with trepidation.

> *Dear Ms. Snow,*
> *I need to speak with you about Jayson.*
> *Please stop by my office tomorrow morning.*
> *Thank You,*
> *Coach Beaufort Biddle*
> *Guidance Counselor*

"What's this all about, Jayson?"

I got a typical thirteen-year-old response. "Nothin.' I don't know, Mom. Biddle's a douche bag. I swear to God, I didn't do anything."

"Yeah right, then why does he want me to meet him in his office tomorrow?"

"It's probably just something stupid. Let's go home, I'm hungry."

"You better not be in trouble. And don't say *douche bag.* It isn't nice."

The minute we got home I knew something was up. Jaycee was curled up on the living room couch and the house was dead silent. No music blaring, no TV— nothing. "Hi, honey, how are you?" No response. I walked over to the couch and saw that she was staring into space. Her normally creamy complexion looked pasty white. "What's wrong, Jaycee?"

Her sapphire eyes shifted toward me and she slowly sat up. It was plain to me then what was going on; we had been through this so many times before. "What did you see?" I asked her.

"A fire. It was horrible, Mom. I couldn't tell what was burning, but it was huge. Smoke was billowing everywhere and I could feel the heat on my skin and stinging in my eyes."

"Oh, honey." I knew that the best thing that I could do for her right now was to just hold her in my arms until the terror faded away. I dreaded these episodes as much as she did. I wish I could lift the burden of these psychic visions from her, but I can't. It's who she is. Besides her good looks and sweet personality, Jaycee possesses one special quality that sets her apart from the other kids. She has ESP. The real thing, scientifically documented. We first noticed it when she was about three years old. By then she had an excellent vocabulary and was very communicative, sometimes too much so. She began making comments and expressing thoughts unspoken by others. For instance, I was sitting in my living room one afternoon and my thoughts drifted back to my days on the Olympic Equestrian Team. I was thinking about one of my teammates. Her name was Sloane Parker, and she was a great rider. We were to compete in the 1992 summer games at Barcelona when my horse, Run of Luck, stepped into a gopher hole and sent me on an aerial excursion which resulted in a broken back.

Sloane and I had become friends while in training, but I lost track of her after my accident. I was wondering whatever became of her when Jaycee looked up at me and said "Mommy, who is Sloane Parker?" I was flabbergasted. I had not uttered her name out loud. How had Jaycee known that I was thinking about Sloane Parker? "What did you say, Jaycee?"

"Who is Sloane Parker, you know, the lady on the horse?"

"An old friend of Mommy's, honey." Shivers ran down my spine. It was uncanny—and it started happening all the time.

Now, having told me of the fire dream, Jaycee was sound asleep. I laid her lithe little body back onto the cushions, and covered her with a cozy throw. I knew she would be better when she woke up.

Exhausted, I dragged myself into my bedroom to change clothes. I had to clean the stalls and feed the animals. That's me: gentlewoman farmer, a muck fork in one hand and a martini in the other. I looked at myself in the mirror. I was looking a little haggard. I examined my skin closely to see if any new wrinkles had appeared. Oh gee, I think that's a new one on my forehead. It won't be long before Botox, but I do have to admit that I look pretty good for 49. Everything has gone a little south, but not too bad. I slipped out of my lavender silk Escada sheath and into jeans, a gray sweatshirt, and Wellies, completing the transformation.

Choosing Wellington to start a new life wasn't a completely random decision. Having no living relatives left in the world, I craved a sense of family to nurture me while I licked my wounds. Dan Gleason—"Uncle Dan" as I used to call him—returned to Wellington after my father's death to help run his family car dealership. Having been dad's best friend, he was appointed my guardian. Dan Gleason was my rock; he helped me to survive the worst tragedy of my life.

Being single at the time, he was in no position to raise a little girl, so he sent me to Andrews Osborn Academy, a boarding school near Cleveland, Ohio, that specializes in equestrian sports. It's where I first fell in love with horses and launched my Olympic career. Knowing that Dan, his brother Andy, and now Dan's wife

Lynn, lived in Wellington somehow gave me and the kids a sense of having "roots" in the community.

The next morning I woke up with a dull headache. The first thought that entered my mind was the meeting I had to have with Biddle. Yuck. I stumbled out to the kitchen and put on a pot of coffee. I did my morning chores, took a quick shower and slipped into my pink cashmere twin set and a Lilly Pulitzer skirt. Lilly Pulitzer always cheers me up.

The school secretary showed me to Biddle's office.

"Hello, Mrs. Snow, please have a seat," he said in a somber tone.

I thought I remembered Crystal telling me that she and Biff Biddle used to date years back—hard to believe. Biddle is a short, stocky guy and has that pro-athlete wannabe look about him. Balding, with watery pale blue eyes—not Crystal's type at all. After a minute or two of small talk he came right to the point.

"I'm assigning Jayson to detention starting tomorrow."

"What did he do?" I asked.

"He wore his spikes into the school building and scratched up the tile floor in the main hall. He knows it's against the rules, but he did it anyway. I guess he thinks the rules don't apply to him."

Hmmm, I wonder where he got that from. "I'm so

sorry, Coach Biddle."

"You won't have to pay for the repairs this time, but on the second offense of defacing school property there is a fine and the possibility of expulsion," he said in a tone that made me feel as though I were being scolded.

Biddle leaned back in his chair and folded his beefy arms. "These kids don't have respect for anything nowadays. They aren't made to take responsibility for their actions. You don't know how many parents I've had sitting right where you are now who deny that their little angel could do anything wrong, even where there's proof positive. And some of them just don't care what their kids do."

I was beginning to feel more uncomfortable than ever.

"Take that business about the ice sculptures— smashed to pieces; ruined the whole festival and those kids did it just for spite."

"I didn't know that anyone got caught for doing that," I said.

"No arrests have been made yet. They don't have proof, but it's pretty well known that the Monroe kid and his cousin Ziggy Haskell had something to do with it. When I had them in gym class they were always getting into some kind of trouble. Ziggy even set another kid's hair on fire. That was an accident, I guess, but he was always getting himself into some kind of mess."

"What happened? Was the child okay?"

"Ya, third-degree burns, but he's as good as new now," Biddle said with a callous tone.

"What makes you think that Tommy and Ziggy had anything to do with smashing those ice sculptures?"

"I don't know for sure, but you got any better ideas?"

So that's how it goes. Never mind the presumed innocent part. Jayson was right, Biddle is a douche bag.

CHAPTER FOUR

"Hey, Ziggy—stop!" Tommy Monroe reached out to grab his cousin's arm, but it was too late. Ziggy threw another Flashback rocket into the air and this time it landed on the roof of Jim Kopeck's barn.

"Holy shit, Ziggy! I told you to keep away from the barn. Now look what you did."

The guys stood staring up at the barn roof and watched as a stream of smoldering black smoke began to rise into the blue-pink sky of the sunset.

"Geez, Tommy, I didn't know I could throw that high," Ziggy whined.

There was no fire hydrant, no water source of any kind they could use to try and stop the flames from igniting. The roof was too high anyway. That barn would be a goner in minutes. Tommy hopped on his ATV, and Ziggy scrambled onto the back. They tore up the hill just as Jim Kopeck turned his blue 4x4 pickup onto the gravel drive that led to his hay barn. He slammed on the brakes. What he saw sent terror through his veins. Flames were shooting up high into the sky while glowing red timbers crashed to the ground below.

"God, no! Not my barn!" Jim shouted to no one. It was way beyond saving, but he heard the siren of

Wellington's only fire truck get louder as it sped toward the scene.

The ATV tires screeched as Tommy braked in front of their trailer, almost sending Ziggy flying off the back of the thing. He was so scared he didn't dare say a word. Tommy flew up the steps and through the trailer door almost breathless. He collapsed on the sofa, his face pale as a ghost. Ziggy went over to the fridge and pulled out two cans of Bud. He popped the first one and handed it to Tommy, hoping that it would settle him down. He'd never seen Tommy so upset.

"Goddammit, Ziggy, I just can't take it anymore. You're going to land us in jail."

"I'm sorry, Tommy. I didn't mean to do it—I swear!"

"You never mean to do it."

"Geez Tommy, don't be mad at me." Ziggy just couldn't stand it when Tommy got mad at him. Tears streamed down his cheeks.

Tommy took a deep breath and another swig of beer. He had to pull himself together. Ziggy couldn't help being the way he was. He was born that way. It seemed to Tommy that *he* was born to clean up Ziggy's messes.

"It's okay, Zig. I'm not mad—it'll be okay. Listen, I gotta go over to Sandy's."

"Okay," Ziggy said as he sank into his Barcalounger and popped the top on his beer can.

Tommy climbed behind the wheel of his ancient Ford truck. There was a full moon that cast a silver glow over the trailer park. It looked almost beautiful. If anyone could make him feel better, it was Sandy. She was the love of his life, and soon to be the mother of his child. He climbed her rickety porch steps and turned the ornate but tarnished Victorian door knob. The foyer was covered with floral wallpaper in shades of pink and green. It yellowed somewhat with age, but was still very pleasing in a shabby chic sort of way.

"Sandy...Sandy, it's me!" he shouted as he entered.

"I'm in here, darlin' ." Her melodious southern drawl came from the kitchen at the back of the house. He could smell the pleasing aroma of something baking in the oven. Sandy was a marvelous cook. She was going to make a great wife. She wasn't showing yet, so she still wore skinny jeans and a tank top. He put his arms around her and drew her close to his body. They kissed deeply while Tommy ran his fingers through her lustrous chestnut hair. How did he ever get so lucky? It was love at first sight when she transferred to Wellington High from Gallatin senior year. God bless Texas.

The timer on the oven went off, and Sandy reluctantly pulled away from Tommy's embrace to pull out a pan of rich chocolate brownies: Tommy's favorite. She loved pleasing Tommy. Never had she been attracted to a man as she was to him. She often thought of the day they met. At six foot three he was hard to miss. Tall and toned with piercing blue eyes and an illuminating smile that transformed his face into pure sex appeal. No girl was safe when Tommy smiled—especially not Sandy Dobrowski.

CHAPTER FIVE

Dan Gleason sat back in his leather desk chair and breathed a deep sigh. The florescent office lighting cast a ghostly pallor to his face, and the mint green Izod shirt he chose to wear this morning did nothing to warm up his complexion. He'd seen hard times before, but never anything like this. News reports predicted that the economy would soon turn around, but Dan saw no evidence of this at his GM dealership. Even General Motors itself was threatened with bankruptcy. If they couldn't make it, how could he and his brother Andy survive? The feds were bailing out big banks and financial companies that were losing billions of dollars, but the little guys like him were left twisting in the wind, hounded by the IRS.

Just as he was pondering the injustice, Andy walked into his office with a cup of hot black coffee for Dan. "I figured you could use this. You must be tired of racking your brain trying to figure a way out of this mess. I know I am."

"Thanks, Andy. You know, I was just sitting here thinking about all the money floating around this valley. Fortunes in trust funds, endowments, and inheritances, and we're going to lose this business over a $100,000 tax debt." Suddenly an idea came to him. "Andy, you might think this sounds crazy, but what if we were to ask one of these local billionaires to make an 'angel investment' and help get us back on our feet?"

Andy looked at him and rolled his eyes. "You are crazy, nobody is going to do that."

"Don't be so sure. We could offer a generous return on investment when the economy turns around."

Andy contemplated the idea while he sipped his coffee. Maybe Dan had something there, he thought. Most of those guys are tight with a buck, but if they see a way to cash in big down the road, it just might work. "Let me think about it," Andy said.

A few days later Dan was dialing Mike Smythe's number. He'd known Smythe for a good many years and had sold him more than one Cadillac. Smythe was heir to a Pittsburgh steel fortune, he was single, having been divorced twice, and his kids were grown up and living on their own. Dan figured that Smythe would be a good bet for an angel investor since he had the money and no one to answer to. Smythe was just the kind of guy who might take a risk if he saw a way to make a hefty profit.

Mike Smythe answered the phone on the second ring and sounded pleased to hear Dan's voice. "Daniel Gleason, it's good to hear from you, to what do I owe this pleasure?"

Dan told Mike that he had an interesting idea that

he wanted to run past him. Was he available to meet for a beer at Joe's? Say around five?'

"Yes, sure, of course," Mike said with a hint of hesitation in his voice. He hung up the phone, and wondered what Gleason was up to. If he thought he could sell him another car right now, he was sadly mistaken. His Eldorado was running just fine, and he didn't have to have a new car just for the sake of having it. Mike changed into jeans and his dark brown leather jacket. Who knew what one was to wear when going to Joe's? He decided to get there early and headed for Grant Street.

He arrived at the bar and was immediately thrown back to the early '60s. He hadn't been at Joe's for a very long time, but nothing had changed. The front room was dominated by a long shiny black bar with chrome fixtures and bar stools covered in turquoise plastic. The gray linoleum floor stretched into the back room, which was furnished with Formica tables and a narrow spiral staircase leading to the second floor. The walls in the back room were filled with huge glass cases like those found in museums. The cases held stuffed and mounted exotic animals of every type. Giraffes, warthogs, wildebeests, mountain lions—you name it. In his other life, Joe was a Big Game Hunter.

Mike perched himself on a bar stool and gazed around at the rest of the clientele. Joe's patrons were mostly old men who appeared to have adopted their bar stools as a second home. A sporting event of some kind was playing on the TV behind the bar, and all eyes were glued to the screen. Mike ordered a Sam Adams just as Dan arrived.

"Hey, Mike, how are you? It's been quite a while." The two men shook hands, and Dan climbed onto the bar stool next to Mike's. He greeted Sandy Dobrowski, who was tending bar, and ordered a Miller. Mike looked around and then gazed upward. "I haven't been here for years, but that elephant head hanging from the ceiling still gives me the creeps."

Dan knew that Mike's usual hangout was the Field & Stream Club, so the culture shock was not unexpected. "It's a unique atmosphere; I'll give you that. So, how have you been, Mike?" he asked.

"I can't complain, wouldn't do any good if I did," he replied.

Dan took a swig of his beer. "How's your Eldorado running?"

Oh no, here it comes, thought Mike. I knew he was going to try and talk me into buying a new car. Greedy S.O.B. car dealers are all alike. "It's running great," Mike said. "I'm going to keep it as long as it gets me where I want to go." He paused for a moment and popped a few peanuts into his mouth. "People today always have to have something new. I believe in getting the most value that I can out of a car, and everything else for that matter.

That's what's wrong with people today. They get bored with something and get rid of it even if it's perfectly fine. They just spend themselves into a hole, credit card debt and all."

Dan saw an opening to steer the conversation his way. "You know, Mike, you're right. This bottomless pit of spending is what got this country into the trouble we're in now. Everyone wants instant gratification."

Mike glanced at Dan out of the corner of his eye, wondering why he would agree with him about needless spending if he ultimately wanted to sell him a car. Shouldn't he be coming at this from a different angle? You only live once, why not have it all, etc. It made Mike even more suspicious. Just what was Dan after?

"Government spending will put us all in the poor house and our kids too," Dan continued." I think that this administration is trying to destroy the economy." Now Dan had Mike's attention. He knew that Smythe was a right-wing conservative and was a political adviser to the Republican Party from time to time. He needed to get Mike talking about how the current administration, with its bailouts and TARP funds, was setting up corporate America for a big crash, allowing the government to move in and take over. Mike bit. He ordered another beer and started in on a good rant.

After they had almost exhausted the subject, Dan brought up the president's cunning strategy to appoint czars to "oversee" everything from education to the automotive industry.

He explained to Mike how the automotive czar was pushing GM into bankruptcy, rendering the entire industry weak and ready for government takeover. And yes, this trickled down from the manufacturers to the local dealers, just like him.

Mike started getting nervous. He wondered where Gleason was coming from, and why he had been invited to Joe's to discuss government policies and the US economy.

Dan soon made it apparent. "You know Mike, because of all this we are having a hell of a time down at the dealership. I know it's only temporary, but we are having trouble at the bank with floor planning, and we been forced to divert funds from our taxes."

Mike took a sip of his beer and said nothing.

Dan continued. "The way I figure it, if we could get some investment money, say half a million or so, we could ride out the storm and pay out some pretty hefty profits after the recovery. I thought you might be interested."

Mike sat motionless, staring into his beer. Dan watched closely for Mike's reaction and could see the left side of his mouth twitching slightly. Red heat began to rise from his neck to his cheeks to the tips of his ears. He turned slowly toward Dan with a snarl, spit out the word

Philistine, climbed down from his stool, and stormed out of the bar.

Dan's jaw dropped in utter shock as he watched Mike's back disappear through the front door of Joe's Bar and Grill. Of all the reactions he expected he never saw that coming. He didn't know Mike very well, but he had been selling him cars for years. Every once in a while he would run into Mike in town, and he seemed like a pretty laid back kind of guy. Dan was only suggesting a business deal, so why did he react like that? Was he psycho? He saw Sandy trying not to look at him from the other end of the bar. His face burned hot with humiliation. How dare that arrogant bastard treat him like that! The burden of despair that Dan had carried for too long exhausted him.

By now it was getting dark, so he threw down some bills on the bar and drove to the dealership, wondering why he ever came back to Wellington. He knew why. His career as a race car driver was over long ago. The day that Jackson Snow flipped his Ferrari on the track and burned to death was the last day Dan ever got behind the wheel of a race car. Jackson was his best friend. He tried everything he could to save him, but it was no use. He carried an unexplainable guilt.

The family had been bugging him for years to come back home and help Andy with the GM dealership. It had been in the family for generations and for the first time since the Great Depression they were losing money.

Andy was a super mechanic, but he was no businessman. Things had been going pretty well for years till the bottom dropped out of the economy. If he didn't pay his trump card, and soon, Gleason Motors was going down, and the Gleason family with it.

CHAPTER SIX

Tuesdays at nine o'clock roll around awfully fast. I'd better not be late for my appointment with Dr. Frick; it pisses him off and ruins the whole session.

"Good Morning, Ivy. Did you have a good week?" he asked.

He always starts off the session with the same question. They must teach them that in psych school.

"Comparatively speaking, yes. Jayson got into some trouble at school. He had to do detention for three days, so I hope he learned his lesson."

"They usually do—eventually," Frick said.

"Doctor, I have something on my mind that I want to talk about other than Bart. You remember my mentioning my daughter, Jaycee?"

"She's the one who has psychic visions, right?"

"Yes. She had one the other day about a huge fire. It really upset her. She said that she could see the fire, but she couldn't tell what was burning. Several hours later, we heard the fire whistle going off. It turns out that Jim Kopeck's hay barn burned to the ground. Well, we thought, *that's that*. Nobody got hurt, thank God, but I could tell that something about the vision was still bothering Jaycee."

"Did she tell you about it?"

"Not until yesterday. She said that something didn't 'gel' with her vision and the Kopeck fire, so she decided to go over there on the off chance that she might learn something, or have another vision."

Dr. Frick shook his head and made a few notes.

"She said that the place was really creepy with the burned out grass and the charred timbers lying all over the place, but she felt no connection. Then, she said that she suddenly did have another vision of a fire, and that she knew for sure that what she saw before, and what she was seeing then was not the Kopeck barn. She still couldn't tell what it was, but it upset her badly."

"I can understand that," said Frick. "It causes a great amount of uncertainty, which results in acute anxiety."

"Tell me about it," I said. When I was a little girl, my father died in a fire when he crashed his race car on the Pocono Speedway. I was devastated. I started having anxiety attacks. I had trouble breathing, I would get dizzy, and sometimes I'd even have heart palpitations. It was scary. Uncle Dan, Dan Gleason that is, was my guardian. He sent me to a psychiatrist who diagnosed pyrophobia. She put me on Valium. I can't take that stuff all the time, obviously, but I still find myself reaching for it when I feel that fear creeping up on me."

"I'm concerned about Jaycee, Dr. Frick. She

worries about when and where it will happen and her inability it stop it—or at least warn people. It's like waiting for the other shoe to drop. I don't know what to do to help her."

"Would you like her to come and talk with me, Ivy?"

"That might be a good idea. I'll mention it, but I don't want her to think that I feel there is something wrong with her, or that she's going crazy. You know how kids are."

"Yes, and it's especially delicate with a person like Jaycee. What else has been going on in your life?"

"Well, let's see—we are getting an intern from Paris at *Equine Style.* His name is Bertrand Reynard. He's actually from Côte d' Ivoire originally. He's working on his PhD in journalism and will be doing his dissertation with us."

"Really? That's interesting," said Dr. Frick. How did that come about?"

"He applied though some government program that the French have and was matched up with us."

Dr. Frick furrowed his brow, but said nothing.

"He'll be coming this afternoon, so I have a lot to do."

"That's just as well. Our time's up anyway. See you next week, Ivy."

Andy was getting ready for another depressing day at the dealership when he heard the sirens in the distance. He knew that Dan had met with Mike Smythe to ask for the loan, and he felt guilty for not going with him. After all, it was his responsibility to try and save their asses too. He didn't really believe that there was much of a chance that Smythe would loan them the money. He never liked that Smythe, and he couldn't figure out why Dan had chosen to approach him when there were a lot of other guys out there who would have been more likely to invest. The scream of the sirens got closer. A cold feeling came over him. He jumped in his truck and headed down Route 42; as he pulled into the dealership he saw hungry flames dancing as they ravaged four brand new cars on the lot. A few feet away from the fire lay the lifeless body of his brother Daniel.

CHAPTER SEVEN

Bertrand Reynard stepped off the train and onto the platform at the station in Jonesville. He was twenty-seven years old, working on his PhD in journalism, and was in the United States for the first time in his life.

A native of Côte d' Ivoire, he was coming to Wellington from the Sorbonne in Paris to intern at *Equine Style*. Although he was born and raised on the African coast, like many privileged young men, he was being educated in France. He had an athletic build. His skin was very dark and his eyes reminded me of melted chocolate. He smiled at us, his teeth glowing white in contrast to his complexion. He wore skinny jeans, a tapered white cotton shirt, and pointy-toed snakeskin boots—a totally European look, complete with man purse. Wow, was Wellington in for a shock. I hoped he would be well-received, or at least tolerated.

I could tell that Jaycee was fascinated. At her young age she had a limited view of cosmopolitan style and living in the Allegheny Mountains did not broaden her vision. Most male fashion statements around here involved flannel, camouflage, and Timberland boots.

"Mom, he's carrying a purse," she whispered.

I explained that Continental men often carried a

satchel and that was no doubt what this was.

"They'll beat him up," she said.

Knowing she was right, I told her that we would suggest that he leave it at home when walking the streets of Wellington.

"Bertrand?" I asked.

"Oui, Bonjour. Mme. Snow?" Bertrand replied in a sexy French accent.

"I am Ivy Snow, and this is my daughter, Jaycee. How was your trip?"

He rolled his eyes and speedily recounted what for him was a horrific journey. It sounded pretty run-of-the-mill to me. Oh no I thought a whiner—a whiner with a purse. We helped him load his bags into my Yukon and headed back to Wellington.

As we drove down Route 30 I kept glancing over at Bertrand, trying to register his impression of the countryside. From his résumé, I learned that he was a city boy through and through. What appealed to him about interning at a small magazine in a tiny rural town instead of a fast-paced publishing house in New York or Chicago? When I asked about that in our initial interview, he replied with some nondescript answer about wanting a totally different environment and learning how "real" Americans lived. I let it pass at the time, but now, after meeting him, the question again entered my mind.

We pulled up in front of the Coach House B&B, his home for the next six months. Roberta was waiting for us on the front porch. Being the curious creature that she is, she was anxious to meet Bertrand and size him up. Roberta was proud of the fact that her B&B had hosted a variety of interns and foreign exchange students. It gave the place an international flair. Most of her guests came from China, Japan, and South America. She had never hosted an African before, and a French African to boot.

"Bonjour, Bertrand," Roberta said. Although she did not speak the language she thought that using a French greeting would make him feel more welcome. Bertrand responded with a rapid monologue in his native tongue which was met with a blank stare from Roberta. It was soon established that English would be the preferred vernacular.

Bertrand unloaded his bags and produced a bottle of Dom Pérignon champagne to celebrate his arrival. Jaycee's eyes grew wide with anticipation, hoping that I would allow her to join in the toast, which against my better judgment I did. We all raised our glasses; Bertrand spoke in his heavy accent "to Ahmadinejad, to Chavez, to Obama. Equality for all!"

My flute hit the floor. A stream of projectile

bubbly spewed from Jaycee's mouth, dousing Roberta's porch swing. Roberta's jaw dropped open. She was speechless, maybe for the first time ever. Bertrand stood grinning ear to ear. What the hell, what the hell did he mean by that toast? Who was this guy? Was he an Al-Qaeda operative? A terrorist? Or just some kind of clueless euro idiot?

Whatever he was, I, Ivy Snow, had brought him to America. Since none of us could think of anything to say at the time, we tried to gather our wits and suggested Bertrand settle in and be ready to start his internship in the morning.

Jaycee and I got in the Yukon and headed back to Little Paddocks, our farm. Mom, why did Bertrand say that stuff about those politicians and everything?"

"I don't know, Jaycee, but we've got to keep a close eye on this guy. Did you sense anything?"

"No," she said. "His purse blew me away. I thought my *gaydar* might be kicking in."

"What do you think now?"

"I'm not sure; I don't have a vibe on him yet."

I parked the truck and we went into the stable to check on the horses.

The next morning I swung by the Coach House to give Bertrand a lift to the office. I decided that my best strategy was to ignore that toast for the time being and concentrate on the internship. I would, however, keep my eyes wide open.

"Good morning, Bertrand," I said. "I thought I should pick you up this morning so that we can arrive at the office together, and I can introduce you to everyone."

"Thank you, Mme. Snow."

"Bertrand, please call me Ivy, everyone does."

We arrived at the office and I installed Bertrand in the room next to mine where I could keep an eye on him. Of course, Melinda, the environmental consultant that rented space in our suite, was the first to swoop down.

"Good morning, Ivy, who do we have here?" she asked in her sickeningly sweet tone.

Melinda was one of those women who came on to every man she saw. She considered herself a femme fatale and made no bones about flaunting it. I introduced her to Bertrand.

"Bertrand is here to do an internship. He's working on his PhD in journalism," I said.

Melinda looked him up and down as if he were filet mignon. Her modus operandi was to project a coquettish demeanor of helpless femininity. It made you want to puke.

She flipped her long chestnut hair (with extensions) and batted her brilliant green eyes (with color-enhanced contact lenses) at Bertrand.

"If you need any help finding your way around

Wellington, Bertrand...I'm here."

She turned slowly and looked back over her shoulder as she sauntered out of the office. I really hated having to put up with Melinda, but the sublet rent she paid came in handy offsetting expenses. Bertrand sported a salacious grin as he unloaded his briefcase.

While Bertrand settled in, I was at my desk getting organized for the day when a phone call came in for me. It was a reporter from the Wellington Herald calling to see if I had any information about a fire at the GM dealership last night. "Oh, my God!" I exclaimed. A fire at the dealership? Dan! I jumped up, grabbed my purse and headed for the door. I had to get over there ASAP and find out what was going on. I called for Bertrand to come with me; he may as well jump in feet first. We pulled into the parking lot and witnessed a tragic scene. Firefighters were dosing the last remnants of charred metal that was once shiny new cars. The police had put crime scene tape all around the lot.

I looked through the large plate glass window at the front of the building and saw Andy sitting at one of the salesmen's desks. He was wrapped in a plaid wool blanket and held a Styrofoam cup with both hands. He stared straight ahead with unseeing eyes. I didn't see Dan anywhere. I asked Officer Fitzpatrick, who I knew from church, if I could go in and talk to Andy. He was accommodating, so I ducked under the tape, Bertrand in tow, and we entered the showroom. I cautiously walked up to Andy, pulled up a desk chair and sat down next to him. His skin was pasty white and his eyes were rimmed in red, from crying or lack of sleep or both. "Andy," I asked softly, "what happened here?"

He turned, looked at me, and breathed a deep sigh. "Dan is gone," he said.

"What do you mean gone?"

"Dan is dead."

I sat in silence for a moment trying to take it in. "How did this happen, Andy?"

"I don't know. When I got here the cars were on fire and Danny was just lying there dead."

My head started spinning.. Suddenly I was ten years old, back at Pocono Speedway watching my father's body being consumed in flames. I could feel my muscles tightening up, and my hands began to tremble. Fear shot through my body as I felt the old familiar pyrophobia kicking in. Beads of sweat began to form on my forehead. I felt a hand touch my elbow, and I instantly turned around. A man in a dark blue jacket and a red Armani knock-off tie stood before me. He was tall and well-built for a guy past forty. He had salt and pepper hair, which hung down over his collar, indicating that a haircut was long past due. His blue eyes were sharp, but I could tell that there was kindness behind them. He handed me a glass of water and gently set me down on a folding chair.

I reached into my purse, found my pillbox, and popped a Valium into my mouth. I washed it down with the lukewarm water, still trying to steady my trembling hands. I sat very still for moments that seemed like hours until the Valium kicked in. I noticed Bertrand just standing in the corner, taking in the scene.

The man who had come to my rescue knelt down next to me. "Are you alright now?" he asked.

I focused in on the rugged features of his handsome face. "Yes, I feel much better, thank you. This is all quite a shock."

"Yes, I'm sure it is. I'm Detective John Garrett of the Pennsylvania State Police. I'll be handling the investigation."

"I'm Ivy Snow. Dan Gleason was my guardian."

"I'm sorry for your loss, Ms. Snow. Is there anything I can do?"

"What happened here, Detective? Was it an accident? Arson?"

"We won't know until we run the forensic tests. We will be contacting Mr. Gleason's friends and relatives for questioning. Here is my card. If you think of anything that might be important please call me immediately."

"Yes, of course I will, Detective." I looked at the card—very official. I noticed that in addition to the phone number for the police barracks printed on the front, Detective John Garrett had scribbled his cell number on the back.

When we arrived back at *Equine Style* the place was buzzing with talk of the fire. Everyone swarmed around us, wanting all the details. I brushed past, and headed for my office, leaving Bertrand to fill them in. I was trying to pull myself together when there was a knock at my door. "Come in," I said reluctantly. This was not a good time to interrupt me. It was Melinda. What did she want?

"Ivy, I need to know exactly what happened over at that dealership," she demanded.

"I can't talk about it right now," I said.

"Well, as you may or may not know, Dan and Andy are my cousins."

Of course, everyone in Wellington is related in some way or another.

"Melinda, I am trying to help Andy. I've got to work on this plan and prepare a statement for the press. We can talk later."

"Later? You don't seem to understand that this is *family* we are talking about. I have a right to know."

"Yes, you do, but not necessarily from me, and certainly not right now." I wasn't about to explain my relationship with Daniel Gleason. The less Melinda knew about my personal life the better.

She spun around and stormed out of the room, slamming the door behind her.

CHAPTER EIGHT

Jail was a hell of a lot worse than Bart ever imagined. No wonder his clients paid him a fortune to keep them out of it. Although he was incarcerated at Rockville State penitentiary, a minimum security prison, it was the lack of autonomy that drove him nuts. He was used to running his own show. He did as he pleased under any circumstances and was incensed by the fact that he, Bartholomew Skeleton, super-lawyer, was expected to follow the same mundane schedule as the great unwashed that surrounded him. He was assigned to farm duty, which was a joke. Bart had never planted so much as a window box in his entire life, and considered anything having to do with soil scut work and totally beneath him. But this was one time that Bart had no choice but to acquiesce.

Each day began with a hearty breakfast of farina, a real departure from his usual eggs benedict or porcini mushroom omelet with hearty slices of heirloom tomatoes on the side. After breakfast, it was out to the fields to toil. Each prisoner was issued work clothes consisting of denim overalls, a long-sleeved chambray shirt, heavy leather boots, and a straw hat to ward off sunburn. In a way it was a welcome change from the standard-issue orange jumpsuit, which Bart secretly thought made him look fat.

The other thing that turned out better than expected was his cellmate. Bart lucked out in that department with another educated white-collar crime guy. Ryan Adler was CFO of the Philadelphia Cosa Nostra. He ran a very successful operation investing the ill-gotten gains of the mob's activities in drugs, prostitution, and loan sharking. Ryan had developed a sophisticated software program that could launder the money to banks in the Grand Caymans and funnel it into foreign investments, thus staying off the IRS radar screen. It was a beautiful operation—a well-oiled machine that gave new meaning to the term windfall profits. Not only did it generate cash flow for the organization in torrents, it afforded a very luxurious lifestyle for Ryan, which in the end was his downfall.

Ryan Adler grew up in South Philadelphia, a primarily lower middle-class Italian neighborhood. Many Italian immigrants seeking a more prosperous life in the New World settled in South Philly, and their families remained there for generations thereafter. Interspersed with the Italians were the Irish, whose forefathers escaped the potato famine in their own country to find refuge between 15th and 37th streets, Broad and Chestnut in South Philly. Ryan was the offspring of one such Irish heritage, and learned early on that what he lacked in brawn he had to compensate for with brains if he were to survive in that neighborhood.

Along with rich culture, fervent religion, and tantalizing cuisine, the Italians also brought along another import to Philadelphia, the Cosa Nostra. The mob quickly established their headquarters in South Philly. The Don from the old country brought his best men with him and then began recruiting young locals into the organization, starting them off in the collections department. Ryan quickly observed that the ticket to making real dough was not in Luigi Suplizio's bakery. Although most of the recruits were of Italian descent, a few of the prime Irish were able to weasel their way in. Ryan knew that he didn't have the muscle to succeed in collections, but something had to be done with the money once collected, so why not earn interest? Ryan convinced the powers that be to let him "invest" some of the profits from loan sharking into a small gambling operation. The idea was so successful that he was able to convince them to take the next step: securities in foreign markets. He was on his way.

With the help of the organization, Ryan was able to earn his BS in finance from Penn and then go on to graduate from the Wharton School with accolades. Not only was Ryan cash cow for the mob, he developed a certain élan which translated to respectability in the higher echelons of Philadelphia commerce. Ryan took advantage of his position and his bankroll to purchase a grand "estate" in a newly-developed neighborhood on the Main Line. It was a six-bedroom, six-bath house in the Tudor style, complete with tennis courts and swimming pool. Ryan didn't play tennis, but the smooth green clay-court surface and taut white nets added to the ambiance of the property. He furnished the house with the aid of Philadelphia's most prestigious design firm, and he hired a cook and housekeeping staff from Sterling. He was all set to be Lord of the Manor; except for one thing—he was missing a Lady.

In the area of romance Ryan was unfortunately at a disadvantage. He had never had much luck with the girls, even in high school. The problem, although difficult to acknowledge, was that Ryan was ugly. He had a weak chin, which he often tried to hide with a beard, a bulbous nose, and then straggly hair, which would soon be gone completely due to early balding. His physique didn't help matters either. He was short, and tended to be on the heavyset side, but he wore custom-tailored clothing which did make the best of an unfortunate situation. All told, it was not going to make securing a Lady of the manor an easy feat. Ryan knew he had to step up his game. He purchased a midnight blue Bentley, and a seaworthy 40-foot Chris-Craft vessel to woo potential women on surf or turf.

His next step was lining up bachelorettes. For

that, he turned to his old friend, *Macintosh*, and joined meetyourmate.com. He concocted a profile that was debonair, yet sympathetic. He needed to cover all the bases. But the most important attribute was to communicate his position of financial abundance. He didn't really care too much about her ladyship's values, but she did have to be a knockout in everything from formal wear to a string bikini. He got his wish.

Each morning before the opening bell rang on the floor of the New York Stock Exchange Ryan checked out his homepage on meetyourmate.com. It turned out that "shopping" for women online was a lot more fun than he thought it would be. Women of all sizes, shapes, and backgrounds paraded before him in pictures and prose. He was looking in the thirty- to forty-year age range. He would have really preferred a young hottie twenty to thirty, but he had to maintain the aura of respectability that he was working so hard to achieve on the Main Line.

The "shopping" had a bit of a voyeuristic quality for Ryan, and he enjoyed that immensely. Who knew what a pathetic lineup of lonely hearts in that age range were looking for Mr. Right. There were fatties, nymphos (tempting), religious nuts, gold diggers, and just plain psychos. But as entertained as he was, he was also frustrated. He'd been on the site for over two weeks and not one potential Mrs. Ryan Adler had appeared—until one Tuesday morning, that is.

Ryan awoke early, stumbled out of bed, (too many margaritas at the club barbecue the night before.) He retrieved the cup of hot black coffee that awaited him in his dressing room each morning, compliments of Consuelo his personal chef. One of the benefits of having a Colombian cook was that she made a hell of a cup of coffee. Ryan slipped on his maroon silk robe over his charcoal pinstriped silk pajamas and lumbered down to his library on the first floor. He headed straight for his laptop and signed into the dating website. He was a creature of habit. Lo and behold, the first potential match that popped up was a very charming and refined creature with a magnetic smile. Her site name was *brownberry8*, and she lived in the next village on the Main Line.

Her profile stated that she was born and raised in the Philadelphia suburb, was educated at Bryn Mawr, worked as a curator at the Andrew Wyeth Museum in New Hope and served on the board of the Bryn Mawr hospital. She was thirty-two, had never been married, and spent her leisure time foxhunting and sailing on the Atlantic. Her photos depicted a very attractive and cultured blonde reminiscent of Grace Kelly, another Philadelphia princess. There were pictures of her in a stunning white evening dress attending a black tie affair; photos of her in full hunt regalia perched on a magnificent Irish Sport Horse, and on the deck of a 40-foot yacht in a swim cover-up that just hinted at the voluptuous body beneath...*brownberrry8* was perfect.

Ryan knew that he had to approach this carefully. He had one shot at getting her to reply to this e-mail, so it had to be good—and it was. He pulled out all the stops, crafting a message that would appeal to her refined sensibilities and entice her to satisfy her curiosity by accepting a date with him. After a few emails back and forth he arranged to meet her at St. David's Hotel for a drink the next evening.

Lydia Brown, a.k.a. *brownberry8*, a.k.a. Sloane Parker, stretched out her long shapely legs beneath the black Empire desk, arched her back, and ran her fingers through her silky golden hair. She reached down and gently closed her laptop, sliding her fingers over the smooth silver case. She had just put the finishing touches on her email reply to *greatmryan007* on meetyourmatch.com arranging to meet him for a drink at the St. David's Hotel. What should she wear for this meeting? A simple black sheath with a gold pendant and matching earrings should project the right image. She had been working on that image for quite a while and was finally getting it down pat. It was one of the more difficult personas to make convincing because it involved a subtle sensibility that wasn't achieved overnight. Much more difficult than a cattle baron's daughter or high-powered politician's mistress. But whatever was necessary, Sloane would rise to the occasion.

Her job was to captivate Ryan Adler to the point where he would be willing to let her in on his Grand Cayman investment scheme. The Securities and Exchange Commission would provide her with dummy accounts to serve as decoys that could lead them through Ryan's money-laundering process to the mob's foreign investments. The IRS was also backing the mission, hoping it would lead to exposing the biggest tax-evasion scheme in recent history.

Sloane Parker was the woman for the job. An independent operative, she hired herself out as a feminine chameleon that could infiltrate the intimate process of any criminal setup and bust it wide open. Sloane did very well for herself.

At five o'clock the next day, she walked into the bar at the St. David's Hotel. It was early, so the bar was empty except for a lone drinker at a corner table. Sloane approached him, and as she got closer it took all of her skills as a top-notch actress to hide her shock. The guy at the table did bear some resemblance to the photo she had seen on the web, and had to be *greatmrryan007*, but oh my God, he took Photoshop to a whole new level. The guy seated in front of her was a troll. She would never agree to go out with him if it wasn't her job. She collected herself, conjured up a dazzling smile, and held out her hand. Ryan stood to introduce himself. He was bowled over. She was even more beautiful in person than on the web.

"Hello! I'm Ryan Adler," he said, taking her hand.

"I'm Lydia Brown, so nice to meet you." Sloane had chosen Brown as her pseudonym because it was so common and could easily result in confusion and uncertainty when conducting a background check. She took a seat at the small table directly across from Adler.

Ryan couldn't believe his good fortune. Lydia would make a perfect "Lady of the Manor" and enhance his image personally and professionally. She'd be great arm candy. Lydia, on the other hand, was going to have to give the performance of a lifetime to convince this dude that she was falling in love with him.

CHAPTER NINE

Three days later I was at the McGonagall Funeral Home
paying my respects to Dan. The McGonagall Funeral
Home is owned by a jerk, someone that I would rather
avoid at all costs. There is a sort of joke that goes around
town: another funeral, another sports car for McGonagall.
I hated going there, but it was necessary. I walked into
the viewing room. It was closed casket due to the nature
of the death, and something even McGonagall could do
nothing about. I looked around and spotted Andy and his
wife, Selena, sitting next to Dan's wife, Lynn. It was
heartbreaking. I approached the casket and knelt to say a
prayer for Dan's immortal soul. Then came the hard part:
facing the living. Lynn looked absolutely devastated. I
could tell that she had been crying for days, her eyes
were red and swollen. I approached the family and shook
hands—it's funny; I don't know anyone who knows what
to say at that particular moment. Even a wordsmith like
myself is dumbstruck. I murmured the general
condolences and slipped away.

As I was heading back to the parking lot, I felt a
hand on my shoulder. I turned to find Andy standing
behind me. He had a look of desperation on his face. "Ivy,
you got to help me," he said.

"What? Help you how? What's going on?"

"The police think that Dan set fire to those cars and then committed suicide. My brother would never do that. I don't care how bad things got; he would never do that to us."

"Andy, of course I'll do anything I can to help, but I can't imagine what that might be."

"Listen, Ivy, there's a lot more to all this," Andy said, pleading.

I felt sorry for the poor guy. "You'd better go back inside. Let's meet tomorrow morning for coffee at the Perk Me Up Café."

"Thanks, Ivy. Nine o'clock?"

"Okay" I said. I had a feeling in the pit of my stomach that I was getting in over my head—again!

By nine that morning the crowd at the Perk Me Up was beginning to thin out. I walked in and spotted Andy at a small round table in the back corner. He had two large cups of coffee in front of him. I made my way over and sat down on a chair facing him. He looked exhausted. "Good morning, Andy, how are you doing today?" I asked in a quiet voice.

"I'm a little better I think, but not much. Ivy, I just

don't know what to do. The police seem to have made up their minds that Dan did this awful thing to himself, but I know he couldn't."

"Is that what Detective Garrett said?"

"He said that the results of the forensic tests weren't in yet, but that I should prepare myself for the probability."

"Well, what do you think happened?"

"I know that Dan was desperate to save the dealership. We owe a lot of back taxes and the IRS is bugging us every day now. They're threatening to confiscate our assets and shut the place down. Neither one of us knew what to do; then Dan came up with this idea to ask one of the local super rich guys to invest some money to keep us going, and then reap a big profit when the market turned around."

"And did he?" I asked.

"That's what he was doing right before it happened. He told me that he was going to meet one of our customers, Mike Smythe, at Joe's Bar and Grill around five o'clock and put it to him then. I'm supposing he went through with it, but I never heard from him again."

"Do you think Smythe had something to do with it?" I asked.

"Yes, I do think he had something to do with it," he said with venom.

"You told the police about the meeting at Joe's?"

"Yes, they said that they would follow up, but I don't know if they've done anything, and I don't think they'll pursue it very hard, considering Smythe is a big muckety-muck around here."

"I know what you mean," I said, recognizing it as a distinct possibility. But Garrett didn't seem like the kind of cop who would let a suspect's social status affect his search for the truth. "Andy, how can I help you?"

"Ivy, I want you to snoop around over there. See if anyone saw Dan and Mike together. Maybe someone overheard something; I don't know—anything to help me prove that Dan didn't set fire to those cars and then kill himself."

"I'll see what I can do," I promised, although I didn't have a clue.

When I arrived back at the office, I headed straight for Bertrand's desk. He was on his laptop doing God knows what. I got his attention. "Bertrand, I have an important assignment for you. We are working on a story about Polo in America, and I need you to research the industry. I'll need profiles of the top teams and players, their hottest rivalries and the high-stakes matches. I want to know what kind of money is spent on this sport and who the big corporate sponsors are."

"Yes Ivy, I can do that," Bertrand replied.

"I want the report on my desk by Friday." There, that ought to keep him busy. I not only needed to keep him busy, I needed to inundate him so he wouldn't have time to do anything else.

I went to my office and found Melinda standing in front of the door. "Good morning, Melinda, how are you?" I asked tenuously.

"I'm waiting for you, Ivy," she snapped. "I thought that perhaps now you may have time to talk to me about what happened to my cousin."

I figured that I'd better get this over with because Melinda would never stop bugging me. When she wanted something she was like a dog with a bone.

"I want to know exactly what happened at that dealership," she demanded.

"I would've thought that you could discuss that with your family, Melinda."

"We are all very distraught, as you can imagine. Everything has been in such an upheaval with the funeral and everything."

I thought back to my visit at the McGonagall Funeral Home and realized that I had not seen Melinda there at all. "I'm sorry to disappoint you, Melinda, but I'm afraid that I don't know anything more than anyone else does about this tragedy."

"Well, isn't that supposed to be what you journalists do? Snoop around, find out what's going on, and then spin it to the press?"

I just stared at her. "Melinda, you obviously don't

have any idea about how the profession works, and I don't have time to explain it to you now. I'm sorry, but I don't have any inside information. See you later." What a nervy broad. She's one of the superior types that think everyone should jump at her command. Sorry sister, I don't play that game. I sat back in my desk chair and tried to put my mind on how I could help Andy.

As I mulled things over, I realized that I really didn't know very much about Smythe. Let's see, I knew that he was heir to a steel fortune, that he was retired from the Philadelphia Press, he lived at Morgan House on East Main Street, and was a member of the Field & Stream Club, blah, blah, blah. That was about it. I wondered what else Google might be able to tell me. Okay, here's something new. It seemed that Smythe had been married and divorced twice, and had three grown kids; that means property settlements, alimony, child support, cha-ching, cha-ching. And it looked like his retirement was not so much a gold watch thing as a kick in the pants thing. He and Hess had some kind of major falling out; ah ha, must be about that embezzlement business, but no details. Hmmm, that was about all I could discover, and I had to get to work on the stack of articles in need of editing.

Just then the phone rang. It was Jaycee. "Hey, Mom, how's your day going?"

"Okay, how about you? What's up?" I could hear

the excitement in Jaycee's voice.

"I just came back from the riding club and all the kids were talking about the fire at the dealership."

"Oh, really, what were they saying?"

"Well, they were saying that the police and everybody think that it was suicide, but there's a rumor flying around that it was murder."

"Did they say who they think did it?"

"No, Mom, but I'm getting one of my strange feelings. It hasn't become clear yet, but I keep seeing these big stuffed animals. Lions, tigers, vultures, you know, what's the word? Taxidermy—like at Joe's Bar and Grill."

At five o'clock that afternoon I donned my Burberry, opened my umbrella, and sloshed across the street to Joe's. If I was going to be of any help to Andy, Joe's seemed like the logical place to start. I purposely went at five knowing that it was the time of day that Dan had scheduled his meeting with Mike. Maybe some of the regulars that were there that day would be there now. People are such creatures of habit.

I slipped onto a bar stool next to an octogenarian who was staring at the flat screen behind the bar. Oddly enough, it was turned to a soap opera, but he seemed to be enthralled. It occurred to me that it might not be as easy to get information out of these guys as I thought it would be. Best start with the bartender. "Hi, Sandy, how are you?"

"I'm fine, thanks," she replied, patting her pregnant belly.

Sandy was one of those girls whose goals consisted of marriage and babies' right after high school, although not particularly in that order. I asked for an Absolut Vodka Martini up with two olives. She served it ice cold, shaken not stirred à la 007. "This is wonderful, Sandy. You sure know how to concoct a martini." She smiled broadly as she rinsed glasses. Maybe if I started out with a little flattery it might warm her up. "Isn't it just awful about the fire at the dealership the other night?"

"Oh my, yes, especially Dan Gleason," Sandy lamented. "He was such a nice guy. He and his brother, Andy."

"Was he a regular here?" I asked.

"Not really," replied Sandy, "but you know, he happened to be here earlier that day. Sitting right where you are, as a matter of fact."

That kind of gave me the creeps. "Was Andy with him?"

"No, he was here with Mike Smythe. You know who Mike Smythe is, don't you?"

"Yes," I said. "But I didn't know that he and Dan were friends."

"Well, I don't know if they were actually friends, not good friends anyway. It's the first time I've seen them in here together."

While Sandy filled another customer's order, I thought about what my next move should be. Suddenly, the old guy next to me spoke. "It didn't look like they were friends to me. Mike Smythe seemed pissed off, and he left Gleason with the check. Cheap bastard."

This guy didn't seem to be much of a Mike Smythe fan, so I hoped that I might be able to get more out of him.

He accommodated me. "I never liked that son of a bitch anyway. There's something weird about him, he puts on a front," he continued.

"What do you mean?" I asked.

"Well, he's got a lot of money, or at least that's what he wants people to think, and he walks around like he owns the town. He tries to act like he's friendly, but I think he'd just as soon stab ya in the back. Gleason looked really upset when Smythe left, so they musta had a fight or somethin."

"Did you talk to him?" I asked.

The old man took a swig of his beer. "No, he left right after Smythe did. I felt sorry for the poor fella."

As I was finishing my drink, Sandy ambled up to my end of the bar. "You know, Ivy, George isn't the only one who thinks there's something weird about Smythe."

"What do you mean?" I asked her

"Don't you think it's kind of strange that a guy in his position would take a job as a school bus driver?"

"What?!" I blurted out.

"It's true," she said. He drives number 27, the middle school bus. My nephew rides it, and my sister was shocked to see Mike Smythe behind the wheel. That's pretty strange if you ask me."

CHAPTER TEN

My cell phone buzzed at six ten. I looked down at an unfamiliar number and swiped the screen.

"Ivy Snow? It's Detective John Garrett of the Pennsylvania State Police. I'm calling about the Gleason case."

I was caught completely off guard. "Do you have any news?'

"Nothing conclusive, but I have a few questions for you, Ms. Snow. Could you meet me at the police barracks tonight?"

"Well, I suppose so. It's kind of short notice," I said.

"I'm sorry about that, but we are trying to get this case wrapped up as soon as possible."

An hour later I was in the interrogation room.. The wooden chair I sat on was uncomfortable, but then again the police are not known for luxury accommodations. Detective Garrett asked all the usual questions: my relationship with Dan Gleason; the last time I saw or spoke to him; did I know if he had any enemies, etc., etc. I filled him in on everything I knew, including Andy Gleason's conviction that Dan did not kill himself, and his suspicion that Mike Smythe was somehow involved. It was Garrett's last question that threw me for a loop. He asked me if I would join him for dinner.

We were seated at a corner table at the Willow Inn. Garrett was off duty, so we both ordered cocktails. I knew that I really needed one, and I suspected that he did too.

"Thank you for joining me, Ms. Snow," he said.

"Please, call me Ivy."

"It's John," he said with a brilliant smile.

He talked about his years on the police force, and about his dedication. Unfortunately, his success left a big hole where there should be a loving wife and family. I detected an underlying sadness in his story. I told him about my father's death, and about my years as an Olympic rider. Then, he asked me the question I dreaded—what happened with my marriage? It was time to come clean if there would ever be a chance for love again.

I suggested that we order another cocktail as we settled in and I told John about my past. I met my ex-husband Bartholomew Skeleton at the Devon horse show outside of Philadelphia. We had a whirlwind romance and soon were married and the parents of twins. Things had been going pretty well up until the twins were toddlers, and then the tsunami struck.

It was a bright, crisp Indian summer day when I pushed the twins' stroller through the door of our neighborhood bookstore. I was there to do a little sleuthing to see what was new in equestrian publishing. I found the right section, and was gazing at various titles, when I caught sight of a woman standing a few feet away. She was a tall lanky blonde, dressed in jodhpurs and paddock boots. She was leafing through a book on saddle seat equitation when she suddenly looked up and caught me staring at her. She smiled broadly, and I could feel the red heat of embarrassment creep up my neck and into my cheeks. "Have you read this book?" she asked, as she turned the cover toward me.

"No I haven't. I don't know a lot about saddle seat equitation."

She took a few steps toward me and handed me the book. I took a closer look at the cover photo of an elegant rider and a majestic horse, and realized that it was her. "That's you!" I said, stating the obvious. She smiled again, and told me her name was Marion Fallon. She had been a three-time world champion at Louisville. She told me that she herself was writing the book on training and showing American Saddlebreds, and was in fact looking for a publisher, and would appreciate any advice I could give her.

The twins were fast asleep in their stroller, so I suggested coffee.

Rittenhouse Books has a lovely little coffee shop adjacent, so we grabbed a table and ordered lattes. We talked about Marion's book and my new magazine, *Equine Style*. Marion told me that she was born and raised on a horse farm near Shelbyville, Kentucky, which came as no surprise considering her melodious southern accent. She spent her whole life training and showing Saddlebreds, and won a lot of ribbons, including several firsts at Devon. As a matter of fact, it was at Devon that she met and married her husband, a Philadelphia criminal defense lawyer.

"Well, that's quite a coincidence," I said. "I met my husband at the Devon Horse Show too, and he's a criminal defense lawyer!"

At that moment, something in the air changed. I knew that Marion could feel it too by the look on her face. We sat and stared at each other across the table. "Your husband, what's his name?" I asked, trying to sound casual. She spoke his name, Bartholomew Skeleton, and I could feel the blood draining from my face. "What did you say?" She repeated his name. I pushed my chair back and stood up "Are you joking? Is this some kind of joke?" I said, barely able to choke out the words. Marion reached into her Coach bag, and pulled out her wallet. She flashed a picture of Bart right under my nose.

"Oh my God! That's Bart...that's my husband, Bart." Marion looked at me as if I were crazy.

I stood up, grabbed the stroller, and flew into the ladies room, heaving. I never felt so sick in my life. What was this woman saying to me? That Bart was her husband too? A bigamist? Maybe I got it wrong. Maybe she said her ex-husband—but my Bart had never been married before. I was his first wife—his only wife! Who was this woman? Why was she saying these things? Where did she get that picture of Bart?

I grabbed onto the sink and tried to steady myself. I felt as if I were going to collapse. This woman must be out of her mind. I had to pull myself together and find out what was really going on here. Marion dashed into the ladies room right behind me. She was ashen. We spent the next few hours trying to piece together an insane situation. Apparently, she and Bart lived in Pittsburgh and he traveled back and forth to Philadelphia on business.

Same story he told me, only vice versa.

Did you ever have your life implode in a matter of seconds? That's what happened to me standing there in the ladies room of Rittenhouse Books. I just could not wrap my head around the idea that Bart was married to another woman—and she was standing right in front of me! Bartholomew Skeleton was leading a double life.

John Garrett's jaw dropped. Whatever he had been expecting, it wasn't this. The waitress approached, and we ordered our entrees. It was the segue I needed before launching into the rest of the story.

I explained that I was trying hard to recover from the shock and anger over what Bart had done to me and to his own children. The S.O.B. told me that he would be attending the Allegheny County Bar Association's annual meeting. He was slated to give several speeches, and conduct a workshop on the latest precedents in rape cases. What he didn't mention regarding his busy schedule was the time-out he would be taking to marry Ms. Marion Fallon.

How did he think he was ever going to get away with it? Upstanding citizen, model husband, and father on one side of the state; romantic fairytale newlywed on the other? It took an ego the size of Texas. That's the thing with narcissists; they actually believe that they are above bowing to the norms of society. They deserve to have more because they are special. They deserve to do as they please. Rules don't apply to them.

Mr. Special came home late that evening, probably after having dinner with Marion, and then making some sort of excuse about having to go into the office to work late on an important case, perhaps even through the night. I wondered if it made him nervous having two wives in the same city at the same time? Probably not. After all, he was too clever to be caught.

"Hello, Bart, how was your day, dear?" I decided to keep up the charade until just the right moment.

"It was fine, Ivy, but I'm really tired."

I'll bet.

"I do have some good news, babe. I've been asked to say a few words at Judge Fitzgerald's retirement dinner tomorrow night at the Union League Club of Philadelphia. We will be seated with the judge and his family at the head table."

"Won't that be nice," I said, feigning interest. I could tell that Bart was especially pleased with himself. Judge Fitzgerald was an important player in Philadelphia, and it was an honor to be in his inner circle. "Ivy, why don't you go shopping tomorrow and buy yourself a new dress for the occasion? Pick out something in emerald green, it's the judge's favorite color."

Great, with everything else I had to do tomorrow, hunting down a new dress. Emerald green at that. Great, just great. Wait a minute, that gave me an idea.

The next evening, I swung by the Hilton and collected Marion, emerald green dress in tow. I dropped her off at the front of the Union League building, parked the car in the garage next door, and phoned Bart to say that I would be detained at the hairdressers.

Marion entered the lavish dining room, which was decorated with huge sprays of green and white orchids, giving it an almost tropical feel. Their scent was heavy in the air. She gathered up the emerald silk taffeta of her gown, glided up to the head table, and stood behind the chair right next to Judge Fitzgerald's. "Good evening, Judge," she said, using her most dulcet southern belle tone.

"Ah, good evening, my dear." Judge Fitzgerald stared at Marion. He was visibly confused. Who was this woman and why was she at his table? "My dear, you will have to forgive me..."

"Judge Fitzgerald, I'm Marion Skeleton, Bart Skeleton's wife," she said, holding out her hand. The judge was dumbstruck. Bart Skeleton's wife?

What happened to Ivy? Bart never said anything about divorcing Ivy and marrying this woman.

Just then Bart entered the room. He was annoyed with Ivy for being late. He hated entering a room alone, especially at an important function like this. He made his way through the sea of tables stopping to greet the movers and shakers of Philadelphia society. As he approached the head table he locked eyes with Marion, who was smiling at him broadly.

"Good evening, Bart," she said. "We're glad to see you're here at last. Judge Fitzgerald and I have just been getting acquainted."

Bart stood stock still. He glanced over at Judge Fitzgerald, who was glaring at him. "Please Bart, have a seat." The judge gestured to the empty chair on his left, and whispered into Bart's ear, "Why didn't you tell me that you and Ivy had divorced?"

Bart was about to start in on his explanations when I chose to make my entrance. When he saw me he sprang up, tipping his chair backward onto the floor. Everyone around him looked over to see what the commotion was all about. Wearing the exact same emerald green gown as Marion was wearing, I marched straight up to Bart and kissed him on the lips. The color drained from his face.

The judge threw his napkin onto the table. "Bartholomew, what is going on? What is the meaning of this?"

Bart backed away from the table, turned, and stormed out of the room. The judge was fuming. The room was awestruck. Marion and I laughed hysterically. Public humiliation of Bartholomew Skeleton—mission accomplished.

CHAPTER ELEVEN

At about the same time, Ryan Adler was also getting his comeuppance. He pulled his Bentley up to the curb in front of the Philadelphia Union League Club, and handed his keys to the valet. If that punk kid got one scratch or dent on his sublime automobile there would be hell to pay. That was the one problem with driving an expensive car. You couldn't be too careful about protecting it from the damage caused by the carelessness of the service class. Ryan was in an otherwise fabulous mood. Things were going well with Lydia. They had been seeing each other for about a month, in which time they attended the opera, the ballet, the theater, and had dined at the finest restaurants in town. Lydia was easy to be with— charming, humorous and accommodating. She let him take the lead and followed the dance of their courtship with style and grace. Another quality that Lydia had going for her was that she had money of her own. Not that Ryan didn't have enough to cover every conceivable expense, but it was reassuring to know that she wasn't just after his money; she was dating him because she was obviously attracted to him.

Ryan felt it was time to take their relationship to the next level, and tonight he had the confidence to move ahead. He asked Lydia to meet him at the Philadelphia Union League Club for dinner. When he made his reservation he told Theodore which table he wanted. Seclusion from prying eyes and ears was of the utmost importance, and he wasn't one to leave that sort of thing to chance.

Sloane Parker put the final touches to her expertly applied makeup. She was wearing a champagne-colored Chanel suit shot through with gold threads, and simple nude Manolo pumps, chosen specifically to portray an image of understated elegance. The perfect ensemble which alter ego Lydia would wear for dinner at the Union League Club. She was meeting Adler at seven, so she had just enough time to check in with Will Sutton, her contact at the SEC. She dialed his number and he picked up immediately, working late at the office as usual. She often wondered if Will had a personal life at all. "Hi Will, I thought I'd give you a call before my *date* tonight and fill you in on my progress."

"I'm all ears," he said. He was impressed with Sloane's professionalism, but he often wondered how a girl in her line of work could ever fit in time for her personal life.

"Things are going splendidly. We are having dinner at the Philadelphia Union League Club tonight, and if I know my mark well, and I do, he's going to suggest that we see each other exclusively."

"Nice work–fast too. What's your game plan?"

"I'm going to act favorably toward the idea, but I won't commit. I don't want him to think I'm a sure thing just yet. I want to introduce the subject of my investments, which I will do before he gets to his agenda. I'll tell him that I know he's a financial genius, and that I need his help. I want to give him the idea that my relying on him is an important facet of our relationship; it will give him a feeling of being in control. I want to plant the idea in his head while he's all hot and bothered."

Sutton considered this. "What about any sexual advances?"

"Don't worry; I know how to handle that," Sloane said with a wry smile. She wasn't expert at this game for nothing.

Ryan was waiting for her as she entered the richly appointed Grand Quarter Hallway.

"Lydia, darling, you look beautiful."

She knew she did, but she blushed slightly, just enough to look demure but at the same time sophisticated. "Thank you, Ryan. It's lovely to see you."

Theodore took them to their table in the 1862 dining room. Sloane had to admit that it was magnificent. She had been to many of the best four-star hotels and private clubs throughout the world, and the Philadelphia Union League Club held its own. The room was elegant, yet comfortable with its burgundy velvet-tufted banquettes and gilt-framed oils of historical significance. The fact that Abraham Lincoln himself had visited here was thrilling to Sloane. Just imagine: Abraham Lincoln and Ryan Adler sharing the same four walls. How nauseating.

The waiter took their drink orders and Ryan puffed up, preparing to dazzle Lydia with his proposal for exclusivity. But Lydia beat him to the punch. "Ryan, I'm so glad that we are dining together tonight. I have a very perplexing problem, and I need your help—your expertise."

Ryan was caught off guard. What was this all about?

"I know that we have never discussed money before, but I'm in sort of a tight spot," she said.

"What kind of tight spot?" Ryan asked tentatively.

"Well, it seems as though my financial planner made some serious errors with my investments. It looks like I'll be facing horrendous tax liabilities this year if I don't do something very clever—and fast." Panic rose in Lydia's voice.

Ryan was silent. He never expected this. The wheels in his head were turning fast. This talk of finances and taxes came out of nowhere. He didn't like the idea of Lydia getting close to his professional life—not yet anyway. He had told her that he was president and CEO of a boutique financial company that kept a very low profile. He had established the firm as a cover for his mob activities, but it was just a shill.

"I know that there are offshore shelters and that sort of thing, but I don't know any way of tapping in to those of avenues. I thought maybe you could help." Sloane covered his hand with hers.

"I... I suppose I could take a look for you," Ryan said. He had a bad feeling in the pit of his stomach. Something didn't feel right, but maybe he was being overly cautious. He was in unfamiliar territory where personal relationships were involved. Besides, he had gotten to know Lydia pretty well over the past few weeks, and his plan was going forward very smoothly. He didn't want to do anything to drive Lydia away at this point. That might happen if he didn't help her out of this mess she was in. She would be disappointed and lose interest in him; he didn't really have a choice. She did look awfully good sitting there with him in the 1862 room. "Why don't you send your statements over to my office tomorrow morning?"

Lydia looked visibly relieved. "Oh thank you, Ryan. I just know that you'll figure something out."

Ryan decided not to bring up the subject of dating exclusivity at this time. He didn't want Lydia to think he was expecting tit for tat.

The following morning Ryan opened the manila envelope that held Lydia's financial statements. Whoa—

she wasn't kidding; what a mess. That financial planner was either a fraud or a kindergarten dropout. He had never seen such a screwed-up portfolio in his life. He would have to set up new dummy investments and then roll these assets into them. He could then liquidate them through his usual channels in the Grand Caymans and filter those into China and India along with his other "client's" investments. Good luck to the IRS finding them then. He'd be a hero to Lydia, and sealing the deal with her would be a piece of cake. Ryan picked up the phone and set things in motion.

As soon as Sloane handed "Lydia's" financial papers to the messenger, she called Will Sutton. "Well, I got things underway," she said.

"Good. How long do you think it will be before he takes action?"

"I think he'll get on this ASAP. He's anxious to push our relationship forward, so I don't think he'll waste any time."

"OK. I'll call Frank Harrison over at the IRS and we can start a trace on those account numbers."

"Good luck," Sloane said. "Keep me posted."

The sting went down like lightening. Once the IRS could follow those dummy accounts they were led all the way down to the Cosa Nostra's interests abroad. It was like dominoes. One fell, and hundreds of others came down with it. Ryan sat behind his desk sucking on a

Cuban cigar when the light on his phone started blinking. It was his secretary, Judy, bugging him, but he wasn't going to answer. He had a grueling day fixing Lydia's mess, and he wanted to search for a new restaurant for his date with her tonight. After a moment, he heard a loud rapping on his door, and Judy burst into the room. "Mr. Adler, there's a man to see you." She was white as a ghost and obviously frightened.

"I'm not expecting anyone, Judy; tell him I'm not in."

A tall guy in a cheap suit barged by Judy, marched right up to Ryan's desk, and shoved a badge in his face. "Ryan Adler?"

"Yeah." Ryan started to stand up.

"I'm Edward Hardy, FBI. You're under arrest for tax evasion, money laundering, and mail fraud. You have the right to remain silent…"

Ryan's jaw dropped in shock. Was this some kind of a joke? He knew it wasn't. It was his worst nightmare come true.

The next thing he knew, Ryan Adler was convicted on all counts and sent to Rockville state prison. Don Geonelli was furious over this development for two reasons. One having to do with financial disaster for the organization, and the second, his concern over Ryan Adler's discretion. As far as reason two was concerned, he needn't have worried. Ryan was no stool pigeon and he had no intention of finding himself wearing a cement jacket at the bottom of a river. He was determined to do as much as he could from the inside to advance the Don's agenda and try to get back in his good graces.

As luck would have it, his cellmate was none other than Bartholomew Skeleton, infamous criminal defense lawyer. Ryan was familiar with his work, since several of Bart's former clients also had ties to the organization. Ryan knew that Bart was someone that Don Geonelli would like to have on his team.

Unfortunately, Bart's license to practice law was in jeopardy at the moment, but consultation work would be valuable as well. Ryan and Bart became fast friends at Rockville. Given the fact that they were the two smartest, most sophisticated guys there, they would make an invincible team. Once Bart learned of Ryan's background he began to consider how the possibilities could help enhance the plot he was hatching to achieve his number one objective in life—getting revenge on that bitch Ivy Snow. Bart was determined to get even with Ivy for what she had done to him. Putting him in jail, humiliating him, and jeopardizing his legal career—his very livelihood. He'd see that she'd pay for what she did, pay with her life. Bart wasn't the only one who had a thirst for revenge. Ryan was determined to destroy Sloane Parker and he had the means to do so, especially now that Bartholomew Skeleton was in his corner. Once they formed their unholy alliance they were amazed to discover how many people they knew in common.

One man in particular rose to the surface: Bart's former client, Michael Tellington Smythe. Bart had learned that Mike moved to Wellington to further Victor Hess's political interests. That was a lucky coincidence, since Ivy chose Wellington as the new home for herself and the twins. Bart's parental rights required that Ivy keep him informed of the living arrangement she made for their children. It would be a cinch for Bart to connect to Ivy through Ryan's associates on the outside. Smythe owed Bart beaucoup bucks for the legal bills he never paid related to his embezzlement case.

Coincidently, the name Michael Smythe also appeared regularly on Ryan Adler's list of deadbeats who owed the organization big-time gambling debts. Smythe had managed to elude collections for months, and now Ryan knew how. Conveniently hiding out in Nowheresville made it easy to stay under the Cosa Nostra's radar screen.

It was time to collect all around.

CHAPTER TWELVE

Sloane Parker made rigid rules for herself and she had to follow them religiously—if she wanted to stay alive. One such rule concerned follow-up.

She made it a practice to always keep close tabs on the perpetrators she put in prison. Most of her cases ended up with prison terms from ten to twenty years, but they often got paroled and were out much sooner. She knew that many of them spent their time in jail for plotting revenge on the person who put them in jail. In about two hundred cases, that someone was her.

As soon as she learned that Ryan Adler had been sent to Rockville prison she hit up her contact there for information on his accommodations. When she learned that Ryan's cellmate was Bartholomew Skeleton she almost choked on her croissant. Of all people, Ryan had to hook up with a crooked lawyer. Not only that, but she knew that Bartholomew Skeleton had been married to her former Olympic teammate, Ivy Snow. Although she and Ivy never kept up with each other after their Olympic days were over, Sloane did make it a point to be informed about her former teammates. Besides, she liked Ivy; they could have easily become friends if their lives had not taken them in such disparate directions.

An unsettled feeling came over Sloane. The combination of Ryan Adler and Bartholomew Skeleton meant trouble for her, and it was highly likely that it meant trouble for Ivy Snow as well. After serious consideration, she decided to pay a visit to Wellington and get the lay of the land. She opened her laptop to Google MapQuest and found the fastest route. She thought about contacting Ivy to let her know about the visit, but she decided not to. It would be better to meet up with her casually. She needed an excuse to be in Wellington, and Google obliged again. The wellingtondwelling.com website listed upcoming activities in the area, and Sloane noted that the Wellington Equestrian Center was sponsoring a mini trial the next weekend.

Ivy's daughter, Jaycee, would be among the participants. Surely she would run into Ivy at the event. Sloane picked up the phone and made a reservation at the Coach House B&B for Friday and Saturday nights.

I helped Jaycee clean her tack and polish her boots in final preparation for the mini trial. She and Pirate had been practicing for weeks, going over and over their dressage test and perfecting their jumps. I was quite pleased with the results and we both had high hopes for first place in the novice green division. There were a lot of riders trailing in for the event, and the Wellington Equestrian Center was expecting a large number of spectators.

Rather than acting nervous, Jaycee seemed to be in a rather pensive mood. That worried me a little; I hoped that it didn't translate into overconfidence. With horses you never know what might happen.

"Jaycee, honey, you seem a bit distracted this morning. Is everything okay?"

"Yeah, sure, Mom."

"Well, you seem miles away."

"I am getting a strange kind of vibe, Mom."

There—I knew it! "What about, honey?"

"I feel like somebody's watching me, I guess."

"There will be a lot of people watching you when you get in that ring."

"I know, Mom, but that's not it."

I've been through this kind of thing with Jaycee many times before, and it always led to something. "Let's keep our eyes and ears open." I had a queasy feeling in my stomach.

The novice green class would be starting their dressage test in half an hour, so Jaycee got Pirate tacked up and headed for the warm-up arena. I followed behind on foot to help her with any last-minute coaching she might need.

They looked good. I found a prime spot for viewing right behind the judge's station and waited for Jaycee to enter the arena. Out of the corner of my eye, I noticed a tall blonde standing a few feet away. She had a Nikon camera, and was focusing the telescopic lens on the center of the ring. I knew that she wasn't with the firm of professional photographers hired by the Academy. They were all wearing green polo shirts with their company logo.

Jaycee saluted the judges and headed for "A." The blonde woman began snapping dozens of pictures in rapid succession. It was distracting me. I hoped that it wasn't distracting Jaycee. My daughter completed a beautiful test and was rewarded with an impressive score. She was on her way to that blue ribbon! She rode over to me with a huge smile on her face. When she got closer, the smile abruptly disappeared. She was staring at the blonde woman. I couldn't imagine what she was thinking.

"Jaycee, what's the matter?"

"Mom, it's the lady on the horse." I looked all around. There were dozens of women on dozens of horses. "What are you talking about, Jaycee?"

She kept her voice low. "Mom, do you remember a long time ago I told you about my vision of the lady on the horse; you said her name was Sloane Parker and that she had been on the Olympic team with you."

I took a closer look at the woman and I realized that Jaycee was right. It was Sloane Parker! I walked up and tapped her on the shoulder. She turned around, and our eyes met. We recognized each other immediately.

"Sloane Parker! I haven't seen you in ages!"

"Ivy... Ivy Snow. How are you?"

We talked rapidly, trying to fill in years of life in just minutes. "Sloane, why don't you come back to Little Paddocks with Jaycee and me? We can throw some steaks on the grill and really get caught up."

Sloane agreed to follow us home, and we spent the next several hours reminiscing about our Olympic days, and our lives since. Then Sloane dropped the bomb.

"Ivy, there is something important that I need to discuss with you." I could sense that something big was coming. The tone of her voice changed, and she looked into my eyes intensely. "As I told you, I've been making my living for the past several years as a sort of bounty hunter. The last case I worked on resulted in a jail term for a Philadelphia mobster named Ryan Adler. He was sent up to the Rockville State Penitentiary, and I recently found out that his cellmate is your ex-husband, Bart Skeleton."

"What?" I was stunned. Just hearing Bart's name come out of her mouth was enough to shake me, but finding out that he was rooming with a mobster who undoubtedly has abundant outside connections sent chills up my spine.

Imagine, Bart Skeleton with the mob at his fingertips. I remembered his parting words to me: "I'll get you for this, bitch."

Sloane expressed her concern for my safety and warned me to stay alert and watch my back. I was beginning to realize that running into Sloane Parker at the horse show was no coincidence.

CHAPTER THIRTEEN

Bertrand decided that he would rather walk back to the B&B after work than catch a ride with Ivy. He wanted to poke around the town a little on his own, and he hardly had a moment to himself since he arrived. All of that polo research piqued his appetite, so he stopped into the Wellington Sweet Shop for a truffle. He hung around the park for a while and eventually sat down on a bench. He was carefully observing his surroundings, especially the people milling around town.

When he came over from France he landed at LaGuardia and spent a couple of nights in New York just to check it out. The scene there was fast-paced and anonymous, like most of the big European cities that he had visited. He realized that while in New York he didn't make eye contact with hardly anyone, except maybe shopkeepers and waiters. He wondered if all Americans were like that, or only big-city Americans.

He got his answer when he arrived in Wellington and met Ivy, Jaycee, Roberta, and the people at the magazine. Everyone was much friendlier and more open here; at least it seemed so on the surface. It was perfect, Bertrand thought. With friendliness and openness often came naïveté, which would make things so much easier.

He picked up his satchel and headed for East Main Street. As he passed by Morgan House he saw an old guy sitting on the front stoop. The man greeted Bertrand. "Hello, young fellow. How are you?"

"I am well," Bertrand replied. The man asked Bertrand if he was a visitor, or new in town, obviously trying to strike up a conversation. Bertrand explained the circumstances which brought him from Paris to Wellington.

"Well, I'm Mike Smythe, what your name?"

"Bertrand Reynard."

"Bertrand, *voulez vous me joindue pour une bière*?"

Bertrand was surprised. This guy spoke French, and fluently. Nice for a change. "*Oui, ca me plaît beaucoup,*" he said, and they turned to go inside.

Bertrand passed through the leaded glass door and looked slowly around the front parlor. It was furnished with fine antiques, mostly mahogany. They gleamed in the afternoon sun. The walls were painted a soft green and were filled with expensive-looking oil paintings. He stepped from the hardwood floor onto an intricately patterned Oriental carpet crafted in shades of blue and red. Smythe invited Bertrand to have a seat on the ivory damask loveseat while he went to the kitchen for the beer.

Bertrand continued his inventory of Smythe's

possessions and was impressed to see a Steinway baby grand in the corner. Across the room stood a tall grandfather clock with fancy Roman numerals on the face, and an intricately carved case. Bertrand practically jumped out of his seat when the clock began to chime, bong, bong, bong. The time was six o'clock. Just then, Smythe returned with two Baccarat pilsners on a silver tray. He handed one to Bertrand, and then sank down into his favorite blue velvet wing chair. Very Ralph Lauren.

"So, Bertrand, where are you staying while in Wellington?" asked Smythe.

"At the Coach House B&B," Bertrand replied.

A picture of Roberta Bristol formed in Smythe's mind. That low-class busybody, he hated her. He tried hard not to let his distaste show on his face.

"Well, how do you like it so far?"

"I've only just arrived, so it's too soon to tell."

"Well Bertrand, if you find that you don't like it there, I have a room here that you could stay in."

Bertrand was somewhat taken aback. He knew Wellington was friendly, but wasn't this a bit much? He thanked Smythe, saying that he would have to see how things worked out.

The grandfather clock chimed six-thirty as they finished their beer. "I must go now," said Bertrand. "Thank you for the beer."

"I hope it will be the first of many," Smythe said.

As Bertrand slipped out the door, Smythe went to his closet to get the navy blue blazer that he would wear for his dinner date with Melinda at the Field & Stream Club later that evening.

When Smythe arrived at the club, he found Melinda waiting for him in the lobby. He went over to her and kissed her on the cheek. She smiled, being careful not to show her annoyance with him for being five minutes late. Melinda had decked herself out quite nicely for the evening. She wore a baby blue cashmere twin set, which brought out the color of her eyes, with a cream-colored pencil skirt and Tory Burch flats to match.

"You look stunning this evening, my dear," Smythe remarked.

I better be stunning, Melinda thought. I have to pull out all the stops to land this old geezer. "Thank you, Mike," she said sweetly as he took her arm and escorted her into the dining room. When they were seated at one of the best tables in the room, the waiter came by to take their drink orders.

"I'll have an Old-Fashioned," said Mike.

"I will too," said Melinda. She really didn't care for Old-Fashioneds, but she thought it would be more intimate if they were drinking the same thing.

"So, how was your day?" Smythe asked.

"Chaotic as usual," answered Melinda. "And to

make it worse, I'm trying to deal with my cousin Dan's death. It's been a nightmare, and that Ivy Snow has been no help whatsoever."

"Who is Ivy Snow and what does she have to do with it?" Smythe asked.

"She's that woman that I sublet my office space from. She's a mean, selfish bitch." Smythe questioned her with his eyes. "I know that she has all kinds of inside information about that fire at Dan's dealership, but she refuses to even discuss it with me."

"What kind of information?"

"Information on the circumstances surrounding the fire. It all has to do with insurance, Mike. If it's ruled a suicide the insurance company doesn't have to pay out. But if it was an accident, or murder they'll have to. I do know that Dan was heavily insured, so were talking about a lot of money here. Dan told me that I'm in his will. I was his favorite cousin, and I helped him with some business issues. Without that insurance money there won't be anything to inherit. I'm trying to gather information to encourage the insurance company to rule in my favor... I mean *our* favor. After all Dan's wife is depending on that money, too."

As they were perusing the menu, Melinda looked up to see Ivy Snow, and her ditzy friend Crystal Prichard heading for their table. Oh no, Melinda thought. Speak of the devil.

"Melinda, I'm surprised to see you here," I said, planting a big fake smile on my face.

"Really, Mike and I often dine here," she replied while placing her hand over his. "By the way, have you met Mike Smythe?" He stood up to be introduced to Crystal and me.

"It's a pleasure to meet you, Mike, although I think we may have met years ago at the News Club in Philadelphia," I said. Smythe looked blank, but confirmed the possibility. We made small talk about the lovely weather and tonight's special. I felt Crystal nudge me on the arm, signaling that she wanted to move on, so we said our goodbyes and headed for our table.

We settled in with a glass of Chardonnay. "I'm glad that we were able to get together tonight. It's been ages since we had a good gabfest," Crystal said.

"I've missed you too. I didn't know that you knew Melinda."

"She's a real piece of work. Married and divorced—I don't know how many times. Now it looks like she's trying to get her hooks into Mike Smythe. That would be a big fish for her land."

So Melinda had been down the aisle before—

more than once. "To whom, may I ask, was Melinda married?"

"Well, let's see. She was married to that lawyer, Richard Kroc. She caught him cheating on her, and finagled a handsome sum from him in the divorce settlement. He was afraid of creating a scandal that would hurt his practice, so he basically paid her off."

"Then what?" My curiosity was growing.

"Then she married Biff Biddle."

"What? You mean Biff Biddle, the guy that you dated—Coach Biddle?"

"Yes, one and the same. After she got rid of Kroc she decided to trade in the brainy nerdy type for biceps and a six-pack."

Crystal sounded bitter, and I couldn't blame her. She had invested a lot of time in that relationship only to have Melinda pull the rug out from under her. Crystal went on, "That marriage didn't last, of course. Biddle didn't pull down the kind of bucks needed to keep Melinda in the style to which she had become accustomed. After she divorced Biff, she ran off to New York and married some stockbroker. That was over pretty quickly, so she came back here to work on Mike Smythe, I guess."

I sat back and smiled. I got just the break I needed: a personal introduction to Smythe. Now I could get the story straight from the horse's mouth.

Snow, Ivy Snow. Mike Smythe sat back in his wing chair and sipped Drambuie, his usual nightcap. The woman looked somewhat familiar, but he was having trouble placing her. He racked his brain. She mentioned meeting him at the Philadelphia News Club. That affiliation had been long ago, and certainly not during one of the most sterling times in his past. He thought back to those days. One particular day stood out; it was when he made that speech to the monthly luncheon gathering. Yes, it was coming back to him now. He did remember meeting her. Ivy Snow. It was Ivy Snow Skeleton then. Of course, she was married to his defense attorney, Bartholomew Skeleton. Meeting her was what gave him the idea of hiring Bart in the first place. A chilling thought overcame him. Ivy Snow recognized him tonight at the Field & Stream Club. She would remember the details of the embezzlement case. That posed a serious threat. No one at Wellington knew about the lawsuit. Victor Hess had dropped charges against him after Bart Skeleton was arrested for bigamy.

Victor was facing a few problems of his own. His divorce from Sheila was an ugly spectacle splashed across the pages of the National Enquirer. She discovered he was having an affair with her housekeeper, so she smashed in his Rolls with a baseball bat, shot out the contents of his prized wine cellar, and kidnapped his golden retriever. To make matters worse, Victor was losing his grip on his political influence with the Republican powers that be in Western Pennsylvania. He needed boots on the ground there. Someone with connections and influence. That's when he made his deal with the devil.

Victor called a meeting with Mike and proposed dropping the embezzlement charges in exchange for Mike's promoting the Hess agenda with Ellie Henderson, the undisputed Queen incarnate of Pittsburgh conservatives. Mike was uniquely qualified for the job considering that his mother and Ellie had been best friends since girlhood. Of course, Mike jumped at the deal. He would have to move back to Western Pennsylvania, but that suited him just fine. He could move to Wellington, which was only about fifty miles from Pittsburgh. He'd live at Morgan House, a property that had been in his family for years. All he had to do was refuse to renew the lease held by the current tenants, which was just about up anyway. He could renew his membership in the Field & Stream Club, and get to work persuading Ellie to see things Victor Hess's way. Not a bad trade-off after all. Having Ivy Snow Skeleton show up was not part of the plan, and that was unacceptable. Something would have to be done.

CHAPTER FOURTEEN

The next morning I stopped Bertrand in the hall as he was making his way back to his desk. "Hi Bertrand, how was your evening?"

"It was good, Ivy. Mrs. Bristol has made me very comfortable. The breakfast that she made for me was very good. American hotcakes with maple syrup from Aunt Jemima."

"Sounds delicious," I said.

Ivy, may I speak to you alone in your office?"

"Of course, Bertrand. Go in and take a seat. I'm going to get some coffee. Would you like some too?"

"No, thank you, Ivy. I am fine."

I returned with a steaming hot cup of Starbucks breakfast roast and sat down at my desk. "What's on your mind, Bertrand?"

He started in, "I was walking home last evening, and a man stopped me."

"What do you mean? I asked.

"He was sitting on the step of his house and as I went by, he called out to me and asked me questions about why I was in Wellington. I told him about the internship, and then he asked me to come into his house for beer. I felt strange, but I did not want to be rude, so I accepted."

"What is this man's name?" I asked.

He told me his name is Mike Smythe," Bertrand replied.

Mike Smythe. He seemed to be popping up everywhere lately. What would he want with Bertrand?

"Ivy, Mr. Smythe said to me that if I did not like living at the Coach House that I could live with him. I found that very strange."

Strange? It was bizarre. Who met someone and then ten minutes later asks them to move in? I urged him on. "What did you say?"

"I said thank you, but I would have to see how it worked out. He said that he wanted me to come back and drink with him again. I don't know if I should."

"Bertrand, you obviously don't feel comfortable, so I suggest you keep your distance. People here are friendly, but usually not that friendly."

"All right, Ivy, but I did not want my rudeness to reflect badly on the firm."

"Don't worry about it," I told him. He went back to his desk to resume his polo research.

This was getting ominous. It was about time Mike Smythe and I got up close and personal. I needed a ruse. I thought fast and came up with the idea of inviting him to be on my antiques auction committee. I could butter him up by saying that I heard he was quite the antiques expert. I picked up the phone and arranged to meet him at the Willow Inn for cocktails that evening.

We arrived at the same time, and sat at a small table in the lounge. The Willow Inn is a lovely establishment perched on a small lake that is populated with beautiful white and black swans. A young waiter approached us, and I ordered my usual vodka martini and Smythe his usual Old-Fashioned. We talked at length about the antiques auction fundraiser, and how important it was to conservation in the area. Mike agreed to join the committee, and lend us his expertise. Lucky us. I attempted to steer the conversation in a different direction.

"Mike, I heard that you met our intern, Bertrand Reynard."

"Yes, I just met him yesterday. Charming young man. It's nice to be able to converse in French with someone. I get so little opportunity here."

"I can imagine," I said. "I didn't know that you were renting out rooms at Morgan House. Bertrand tells me that you invited him to be a tenant."

"Well, I'm not really renting out, but I thought the boy might be happier at my place. That Roberta Bristol can be, ah, challenging at times."

"Mike, it's very kind of you to offer, but I made a commitment to Roberta Bristol that Bertrand would be at the Coach House for the entire six months of his internship. It would be unfair to her if we made a change."

"Of course," Mike said. "I only offered as a hospitable gesture."

We discussed a few more topics of interest in Wellington: zoning, Mike's pet peeve about the color of the Coach House, the downturn of the economy and how tough it is to do business here. "Speaking of that, wasn't it a shame about what happened at the GM dealership? I understand that you and Dan Gleason were friends," I said.

"Well, I certainly knew him, bought a number of cars from him over the years, but I wouldn't go so far as to say we were friends. Friendly business acquaintances is more like it."

"Hadn't you been at Joe's with him earlier on the evening of the tragedy?"

"Yes," Mike replied, looking surprised that I should ask. "We ran into each other there and had a quick drink. I had to rush off though, because I had other plans for the evening."

This was getting me nowhere. Obviously, Smythe was aware that a number of people saw him and Dan drinking together at Joe's, so he couldn't deny that. He just had to make it well understood that he was there for a quick drink and that he had other plans for the evening. Andy would be disappointed that I wasn't able to come up with more information by now. I decided to wait and call in a day or so. Maybe something else would turn up by then.

Mike hurried back to Morgan House. He didn't have a lot of time to spare after wasting so much of it with Ivy Snow. Her and her stupid committee. None of those dweebs have the money or the taste to invest in any antiques of importance. Oh well, he'd play along with it anyway. It was good for his image to appear supportive of community fund-raising projects. When he got home he headed straight for his bedroom, and his special armoire. He had purchased the magnificent piece of furniture on his last trip to France, and never stopped marveling at the intricately carved satyrs that graced the front of each door. Now, there was an antique worth possessing. He kept the armoire locked at all times. He didn't want anyone to know what was kept inside, especially his nosy cleaning lady, Betsy Quinn.

The armoire contained the essence of Mike's private world. A world he shared only with select intimates. He alone knew the lock's combination, and he ever so carefully turned the tumbler back and forth until he heard the sweet sound of the click. He opened the door and gazed at the collection of exquisite evening gowns before him. The red satin Valentino with the signature bow, the mocha velvet Carolina Herrera, and his pride and joy, the vintage black sequined Yves St.

Laurent. He procured most of his collection in Europe, but sometimes he just couldn't resist ordering something special from Neiman's or Saks.

Mike was known throughout his circle for having an incomparable taste level. Tonight was a very special night, when new potential members were introduced to the group. It was always the most promising opportunity to meet new partners. He would choose to wear the vintage Yves St. Laurent, and indulge in his most flamboyant cabaret makeup—just for fun. He selected a dazzling crystal minaudière in the shape of a tiger and prepared to depart for his friend's mansion, Blue Heaven, where tonight's party would be held. He had to be very careful not to be seen leaving, or there would be questions asked about the mysterious woman visiting Morgan House. Mike locked the front door and gingerly negotiated the back stairs to the garage. Not easy in stilettos!

Just as he was leaving, Roberta Bristol leaned out her kitchen window next door to retrieve a pie cooling on the sill. She spotted a woman teetering on the steps and almost dropped the pie. Who was that huge, hulking woman at Morgan House? At that moment, she realized that it was no woman. It was Mike Smythe—in drag! She laughed until tears ran down her face, and then picked up the phone to call her sister in Scranton. Edna would be hysterical!

CHAPTER FIFTEEN

Crystal Prichard locked the front door to her office and stepped out into the invigorating fresh air. She breathed in deeply, hoping that it would inject her with the strength needed to keep her from drowning in despair. The last call of the day was the coup de grâce. Crystal had spent the entire weekend showing houses to a couple from New York who were hoping to find a country retreat from their hectic city lives.

The Blackstones: Richard and Ramona. He was a Wall Street go-getter, and she, a psychiatrist. Two high-pressure fields that wore them down. On the positive side, they were two very lucrative professions, which would provide plenty of money to spend on a country estate.

Beginning early Saturday morning, through late Sunday afternoon, Crystal ushered them through every suitable property near Wellington. They were critical of everything, and they just didn't understand that out in the country water came from wells, and driveways were often dirt or gravel. Finally, they both showed interest in the Crawford place. It made sense. The Crawfords were also from New York, and had installed every imaginable amenity as soon as they bought the house. It had the requisite Jacuzzi, wine cellar, and home theater—everything a New Yorker needed to "rough it" in the country.

Unfortunately for the Crawfords, a labor relations problem brought their manufacturing plant to a screeching halt, along with their cash flow. They were forced to sell. Fortunately, Crystal had the listing, which meant that she wouldn't have to split the commission with another agent. She hoped that the Crawfords' misfortune would be the Blackstones' dream come true, and that would be the solution to her financial problems.

It was all looking pretty good until five minutes ago, when Crystal's phone rang. It was Ramona Blackstone calling with disappointing news. It looked as though the Blackstone marriage was at an end. She explained that they thought that buying a country house would mean more time to work on their relationship. But on the twelve-hour car trip to and from Wellington, they did nothing but fight. They finally came to the conclusion that no country house would save their marriage. They came to grips with the fact that they hated each other, and that was that.

Oh great, thought Crystal; they couldn't have realized that they hated each other before running me ragged all weekend. No Crawford sale, no Blackstone purchase, and no big fat commission check. She felt like shit. There was only one thing that would help her feel better, and that was a good bitchfest with her best friend, Ivy. She whipped out her cell phone and hit the speed dial which would summon her BFF.

"It's unbelievable, Ivy. Not only am I missing out on the Blackstone commission, but the Crawford deal too. You know what this means?"

"Yes," I said. I knew that it meant a tough decision for Crystal; hold tight, or abandon the sinking ship. "What can I do to help?" I asked.

"Meet me at the Tavern and we'll get shitfaced," she said.

CHAPTER SIXTEEN

Melinda plopped herself down on her ice white Roche Bobois sofa and scanned her view through the floor to ceiling windows looking out over the Allegheny Mountain vista. She lit a cigarette. Melinda didn't smoke in public. It looked uncool these days, but at home the sterling silver cigarette box on her Lucite cocktail table was always full. Smoking helped her think, and she had a lot of thinking to do. She had been walking around the last few days with an unsettled feeling. A nagging in the back of her brain told her that something was wrong. She hadn't heard from the insurance company yet about the settlement of her cousin Dan's policy, and without that money she would have a serious problem.

Andy was acting very strangely toward her since Dan's death. Admittedly, she and Andy had never been as close as she had been with Dan, but still, they were family. Maybe he was angry that she would be getting part of the insurance money. Especially since he must have realized that she would not be investing any of it in the dealership. He never even wanted to talk about Danny's death...not even the will. And what was he doing with Ivy Snow? She spotted them at the Perk Me Up the other day, and she saw Ivy's car parked in front of the dealership several times. It wasn't a GM vehicle, so she wasn't there to get it serviced. Was Andy talking to Ivy about the will? Was she helping him figure out a way to cut her out of the inheritance? She'd put nothing past that busybody bitch.

Melinda arose from the sofa and crossed the room to her bar. She poured herself a stiff scotch and considered the problem. Not only is Ivy in Andy's business, but she's constantly hovering over Bertrand. True, he is her intern, but she treats him like she owns him. She's over at his desk at least a dozen times a day, spying on him, no doubt. I'll bet she goes through his desk drawers at night. Probably his laptop too, unless he takes it home with him. What does she suspect? The way she sneaks around the office, she might have seen something. Maybe that brat daughter of hers said something. What's her name? Jaycee, that's it—talk about spooky. That kid lurks around poking her nose into everybody's business, and I'll bet she runs and tells her mommy everything she sees and hears. There's something else about that kid. It's like she has a sixth sense or something. Whatever it is, it can't be good. Jaycee needed to be watched very carefully.

Melinda climbed the stairs to her bedroom. They were carpeted in ivory Stark carpeting which continued into the master suite. She shimmied out of the fuchsia sheath she had worn to work that day, and slipped into her cream-colored cashmere robe. She closed the heavy silk draperies, and sunk into her down-filled chaise lounge. Her thoughts turned to Michael Tellington Smythe. Mike—the most likely candidate to satisfy her needs in this godforsaken town. Sure, he was a little pudgy, a little bald, but also more than a little loaded. After all, she had a lot of needs.

What did Ivy Snow want with Mike? She put on that big act the other night at the Field & Stream Club, pretending that they had been acquaintances back in Philadelphia. It was obvious that she was trying to strike a common chord. She'd probably realized by now that there are few eligible men in Wellington with his kind of resources.

And what about Ms. Ivy Snow herself? What about her background? What about her past? Rumor had it that she was married to some hotshot lawyer in Philadelphia. What happened to him? She was supposed to be some kind of fabulous horsewoman—Olympics even. What was she doing in tiny Wellington, Pennsylvania? She's after something, that's for sure, and I'm going to find out what it is, Melinda thought.

Crystal's phone rang promptly at nine o'clock the next morning. "Wellington Realty, Crystal Prichard speaking."

"Good morning, Crystal dear. It's your old pal Melinda."

Old pal Melinda? Crystal froze. It couldn't be. What did she want? "Hello Melinda. What can I do for you?" she said, bursting with curiosity laced with dread.

"Crystal darling, I'm calling to enlist your help. As you probably know, I've taken up horseback riding. I just love the sport, and I've decided to get more involved. Of course, that means having a horse farm—at least twenty acres minimum. You're the best agent in town, so of course I'm calling you."

"Oh! Okay." Crystal was almost speechless.

"Now that means that I will also want to sell my current residence."

"Of course," Crystal said, her head spinning. Melinda. OMG, she's the one that stole Biff right out from under my nose. She's a first-rate bitch, and she's a major thorn in Ivy's side. But I am a professional, I have to at least hear her out. I don't have to sign any contracts. I don't have to get involved. Even as the words were forming in her brain, she knew that she was lying to herself.

"When can we meet?" Melinda asked.

"Uh, tomorrow? Ten in the morning?" She couldn't believe that the words were coming out of her mouth. "I'll come over to your place, and we can go over the details." She slowly hung up the phone. What was she getting herself into? Melinda was nothing but trouble. Her latest escapade ended up making Melinda's own brother look like a fool. Her brother, Randall, and his wife, Jillian, had recently separated. Jillian made no secret of the fact that she left him because of his drinking. Melinda was not about to let that go, so she talked Randall into filing a lawsuit against his wife, claiming that she had tricked him into marrying her so that she could get her hands on his family's money. The suit alleged that Jillian and her former husband, some British bloke, agreed to a sham divorce so that she could go after Randall, bilk his relatives, then return to the Brit and ride off into the sunset. It was like the plot of a bad made-for-TV movie. The newspapers had a field day with it, and Melinda even posted the articles on Facebook. Unfortunately for Randall, the readers' consensus was that he was an idiot. Melinda was probably the one that drove him to drink in the first place.

CHAPTER SEVENTEEN

Crystal rang Melinda's doorbell at ten o'clock the next morning. She had decided to spare Ivy the details of her conversation with Melinda. After all, she hadn't made any commitments, and she probably wouldn't, so why kick up the dust? Melinda opened the door wearing a red Escada suit; she would be going to the office directly after meeting with Crystal.

"Good morning, Crystal dear. Please come in," she said, injecting a melodious tone into the invitation.

"Hi Melinda," Crystal said tentatively. She quickly glanced through the foyer into the living room. Wow, the whole place was white. White walls, white furniture, even the hardwood floors were pickled white. The décor was sparse, and ultra-contemporary, especially the large Jackson Pollock-style painting hanging over the fireplace. Was the splattered work a Pollock look-a-like, or the real thing? With Melinda, you never knew for sure.

As Melinda led her into the living room, she asked Crystal if she would like coffee.

"Yes, black please."

Melinda lifted the silver Georg Jensen coffeepot from its matching tray and poured the hot liquid into a delicate gold Herend cup. Crystal didn't dare take the cup for fear that her hands would shake and she would spill coffee all over the white sofa. Melinda set the cup down on the table as Crystal pulled her notebook out of her briefcase.

"As I mentioned on the phone yesterday, I am in need of a suitable horse farm not too far from town. I'll need at least twenty acres and a stable," Melinda said with a sickeningly sweet smile on her face.

"There are a few available properties that may interest you," Crystal said, thinking of the Crawford place in particular. "How quickly were you thinking of buying?"

"As soon as possible,' Melinda said. We'll have to put this place on the market and hope it sells quickly. I wouldn't want to carry two mortgages."

"Of course not," Crystal said, knowing that she was being railroaded.

I'm so passionate about riding. I have my eye on a magnificent thoroughbred over at the Wellington Equestrian Center, and I must find the perfect home for both of us. Your friend, Ivy Snow, she rides, doesn't she?" Melinda asked, knowing full well that Ivy had been an Olympic contender.

"Yes, she was on the U.S. Equestrian Team a few years back."

"She might be able to give me some advice about what to look for in a good stable. I'll have to ask her next time I see her around the office."

Oh no, thought Crystal. Melinda will open her big mouth and tell Ivy that I'm her agent. I wouldn't do it in a million years, but I can't let my business go under. It's a matter of life and death. "Ah, I can research that for you...it's part of my job," Crystal said. She felt like a Benedict Arnold.

Splendid, thought Melinda. Now she knew that Crystal did not want Ivy to know that they were working together. She was hoping that the whole thing would be kept secret. Hmm, interesting position. I bet I'll learn all kinds of useful things, she thought. "You know, Crystal, I was thinking about when I introduced Ivy to Mike Smythe at the club the other evening. She mentioned that she knew him when they both lived in Philadelphia. Mike never mentioned it. Did Ivy share the details with you?"

OMG, it's starting already—the ulterior motive. I knew that there had to be one, thought Crystal. She's pumping me for information about Ivy. "No, she didn't say anything more to me about Mike Smythe."

"Well, she might not want to reveal the details of their relationship. After all, Ivy was married when she lived in Philadelphia, wasn't she?"

Crystal nodded her head.

"Yes, I had heard that she was married to a lawyer, right?"

"I guess so," said Crystal. "I didn't know Ivy back then. I only met her when she first came to Wellington."

"He must have died, or she divorced him, or whatever. He isn't here, is he now?"

"No, I don't know what happened to Bart Skeleton." Crystal's hand flew up to her mouth. She realized that she had just told Melinda the name of Ivy's ex-husband. Now the shit would hit the fan.

Melinda signed the real estate contract, and Crystal headed for the door, anxious to be out of the spider's web. "Uh, I'll set up some appointments for you to view properties. I'll call you."

"That's fine, dear." Melinda's mind was already off real estate and on to Bart Skeleton.

I was working from home when Crystal knocked on my door. I knew immediately that something was up. Crystal never just drops in for a visit. "Hi, Crystal. What a nice surprise."

"Ivy, I need to talk to you about something that happened."

"What happened?"

"I made a big mistake. I agreed to help Melinda sell her house and buy a horse farm."

"You what?" I said, unable to hide the shock in my voice.

"Oh, Ivy, I feel awful. You know how rough things have been with my business lately. I might even be going under. Yesterday, I got a call from Melinda right out of the blue. She said that she is taking up riding and wants to buy a farm. She's putting her current house on the market, and she gave me the listing. Ivy, you know that I'd never agree to work with that psychopath if I wasn't desperate for the money."

I just sat quietly for a moment letting it all sink in. Crystal was in a terrible situation. She wanted nothing to do with Melinda after what happened with Biff, but she was still willing to swallow her pride. I couldn't begrudge her the chance to save her business, even if I thought there was something fishy about this whole thing. It was a complete lifestyle change for Melinda. She traveled so much for her job; I wondered why she would want to be tied down to a horse farm? I guessed she would hire a farm manager. I couldn't see Melinda mucking out stalls herself, so why was she doing this? Wait a minute, I thought; this was the perfect opportunity for me to keep tabs on Melinda. She kept bugging Andy about that insurance policy, and she seemed overly interested in Bertrand's comings and goings.

"Crystal, don't worry about working with Melinda. You've got to do what you've got to do. This way, you can keep an eye on her for me."

"Yes, I can, can't I?" she said with a sigh of relief.

CHAPTER EIGHTEEN

The next morning, Jim Kopeck pulled his blue Chevy pickup truck next to the stable at Little Paddocks. He was making his usual monthly delivery, bringing hay stored in a neighbor's barn. His profits were going to be cut way back this year because of the fire at his own place. He knew he should have kept up the insurance payments on that property, but cash was really tight and he thought it was worth the risk. Now it would take years to build up his business to where it had been just last week. Damn kids.

He heard a door slam and looked around the corner to see Jaycee bounding out of the house, heading toward him. She was a cute kid, and he enjoyed talking to her while he worked.

"Hi Mr. Kopeck," she said. "It's good to see you, how have you been?"

"I've been fine," he lied.

"I heard what happened to your barn. I'm awfully sorry."

"Yeah, it was pretty bad. I lost it all, not a timber left."

"Did they catch whoever did it?" Jaycee asked.

Jim stopped taking the hay bales out of the truck

and paused for a moment to wipe his brow. "No, they didn't catch anybody, but I know who did it—that Monroe kid and his cousin Ziggy Haskell."

"How do you know for sure?"

Jim resumed unloading the truck. "Because I saw them."

"You saw them? Why didn't you turn them into the police?"

"I can't go to the police, not yet anyway," Jim said. "I don't have any proof. It was dark out that night, and they'll claim that I couldn't see clearly enough to make an identification. I know Monroe did it all the same. It's just a matter of time till I can prove it."

"That's a shame, Mr. Kopeck. That was a nice barn."

"It wouldn't surprise me if those two had something to do with the fire at the GM dealership," Jim said with malice in his voice.

Suddenly, a funny feeling came over Jaycee. She could see fire in her mind's eye. It raged as flames leapt into the sky, and sirens screamed in the distance. Something was being consumed by fire, but it wasn't a barn.

Jaycee pulled out her cell phone and sent a text message.

Mom, I need to talk to you.
What about?

About the fire...can I come to the office?
Okay.
Jaycee asked Mr. Kopeck for ride into town.

At the office, Jaycee waited until I finished my phone conference.

"I really need to talk to you, Mom; it's important."

"Sure honey. Let's talk at lunch. How about Joe's?"

"Great! I love their burgers."

"I'll be just a moment," I said.

Jaycee immediately pulled out her iPhone and went to Facebook. There was never any downtime for teenagers. It was important to keep up with what was going on, and she had plenty of news to share as well.

I needed to freshen up, so I grabbed my purse and headed for the ladies lounge. As I passed by the lunchroom I noticed that the door was almost completely shut. That's strange, I thought. I peeked through the crack and saw Bertrand and Melinda in a passionate embrace. Oh, my God! What was going on here? What should I do? Should I confront them? They were consenting adults; at least they certainly looked consenting. I made a split-second decision and quickly headed back down the hall. Bertrand is my intern, but I had no right to interfere in his personal life. I couldn't believe they would behave like that in the office. You'd think they'd know better. And what about Melinda? I thought she had her cap set for Mike Smythe. Is she in a relationship with Bertrand, or was this just a little recreation on the side? My head was spinning. This was too big a mare's nest to unravel now. I caught up with Jaycee and we left for Joe's.

Tommy Monroe was working the lunch shift. He seated us in the back and handed us menus. Jaycee ordered her favorite Joe's Jungle Burger, and I ordered a garden salad. "What did you need to talk to me about, honey?" I asked her.

"It's about those fires, Mom. First Mr. Kopeck's barn, and now the dealership. Something is terribly wrong here. I keep getting visions of horrible fires burning everywhere, but I can't tell what's burning."

"Oh, honey," I said. "This ESP can be a blessing and a curse." Our food arrived just then and Jaycee dug right in.

"I'm scared, Mom. I don't know if the fires I'm seeing happened in the past, or if they're going to happen in the future."

"Jaycee, I wish I could help you, sweetheart." But in this case, I was truly helpless.

"Mom, there's another thing. I think there's something going on between Bertrand and Melinda."

Oh no, I thought. I hope Jaycee hadn't seen any of

their office antics. "What do you mean?" I asked.

"I don't know, Mom, but whenever I see the two of them together, I sense a pink aura around them. I see a river with many bridges, and the air smells like lavender. What do you think it means?"

I didn't want Jaycee to know about the scene I had just witnessed in the office, so I made light of it. "Maybe Bertrand is dreaming up a story of some kind. Who knows?" This kid had enough on her mind without having to worry about Bertrand and Melinda.

All of a sudden, the color drained from Jaycee's face. "Honey, are you okay?" I asked.

"Mom, I don't feel so well. It's my stomach. I think I'm going to throw up!"

I rushed Jaycee to the ladies room and into the nearest stall. She was breathing heavily and making horrible retching sounds. My poor baby. "Jaycee, are you all right in there?"

"Mom, I'm sooo sick!"

"Take it easy, honey, you'll be okay." I waited for what seemed like an eternity, and called her again. "Jaycee, are you all right?"

"No, Mom," she choked out,

I decided I'd better get medical help. "I'm going for help, Jaycee. Hang in there."

I grabbed the door handle and pulled. Nothing happened. The door stayed firmly shut. Was it stuck? I didn't remember locking it when we came in. I tried turning the deadbolt and still nothing happened. It was locked from the outside. Oh, my Lord! I banged on the door with both fists." Tommy, Sandy, help! We're trapped in here," I screamed. I couldn't hear a sound outside. Damn, I realized that I'd left my cell phone in the office. Jaycee called from inside the stall, "What's wrong, Mom?"

"The door is stuck!" I yelled.

Jaycee came out of the stall, her face pasty white. "Let me try, Mom." She pulled on the handle, but nothing happened. Sniff... Sniff. "Mom, what's that smell?"

I stopped pounding and inhaled deeply. Oh, my God! It smelled like smoke. Jaycee and I looked at each other. At that moment we both realized that we were in very serious trouble. Jaycee ran back into the stall and threw up. When she came out, her skin had that clammy look; her eyes were brimming with tears. "What are we going to do, Mom?"

"We have to keep hollering for help." I noticed faint curls of smoke wafting up into the room from the crack under the door. The smell was becoming more pungent by the minute, and my eyes began to burn. I took off my scarf and soaked it under the tap. I wrapped it around Jaycee's nose and mouth like a bandit. "Here honey, this will help." I sensed panic coming over her as I fought to keep it back myself.

I stood very still and tried not to breathe as I

racked my brain for a way out of this. Above all, I had to keep calm for Jaycee's sake. Keep calm? I've never been so scared in my life! I had visions of flames dancing up into the ladies room from beneath the door. I tried the handle again. It was so hot I burned my hand. I screamed in pain, and saw an image of dad's Ferrari ablaze, his face full of agony and fear. Suddenly the whole room went black. The fire must have short-circuited the fuse box. There were no windows in the bathroom, and I couldn't see anything. I tried to keep my breathing as shallow as possible. I couldn't risk hyperventilating. I was losing control. Fire had taken my father from me. It wasn't going to take my daughter, too. I heard a distant sound. It was a siren! It was getting closer. The fire department! Please God, let them find us before it's too late! I was holding Jaycee, with her face pressed into my chest to keep as much of the wretched smoke out as possible. I felt her growing weaker in my arms. I gently set her on the floor where she slumped into a ball. I started banging on the door and screaming again. Dear God, help us! My throat was raw, and I was taking in too much smoke. I began to feel faint when the door gave way and I fell into the arms of a firefighter. I gasped, "My daughter... she's in there!" He passed me off to the fireman behind him and bolted into the room to find Jaycee.

Seconds later he ran out carrying her in his arms; she was gray and limp. He placed her on a stretcher and put an oxygen mask over her face. The paramedics lifted her into an ambulance and helped me climb into the back with her. I was given an oxygen mask as the ambulance pulled into the street, siren wailing.

CHAPTER NINETEEN

The emergency room at St. Ann's Hospital was chaos. Right before we arrived, an ambulance brought in three kids that flipped their truck over on Route 429. It's a dangerous road and more than one kid with a few beers in him, feeling invincible, has met a tragic fate. The paramedics unloaded Jaycee from the back of the ambulance onto a stretcher and took her inside. By then, I had recovered completely except for the burns on my hand. I tried to keep it together. The last thing Jaycee needed right now was a hysterical mother. The nurse in charge directed the paramedics to take Jaycee to triage. I scuttled along behind, every step a prayer. They hooked her up to a heart monitor and drew blood. She was still unconscious, but it looked as though she was gaining a little color in her cheeks. The nurse scribbled information on her chart and hung it on the front of Jaycee's bed. "Ms. Snow, the doctor will be in soon," she said. In the meantime, she dressed and bandaged my hand.

I waited for what seemed like an eternity. Finally, a young man came into the room dressed in green scrubs. He had a stethoscope around his neck, so he must be the doctor. He looked so young. I was amazed that he was old enough to graduate from high school, let alone medical school. He greeted me and then picked up Jaycee's chart and studied it carefully. He approached her and lifted each of her eyelids, shining a laser-like light onto her pupils. I waited in silence, giving him the time he needed to make his evaluation. He looked at me and said, "Her vital signs are good. The breathing is still a little shallow. We are going to have to x-ray her lungs to make sure that there's no tissue damage."

"She's going to be okay?"

"That's what we'll find out," he said.

I got up and walked over to Jaycee's bedside. I watched her chest move up and down. My baby. As I took her hand, her eyelids began to flutter as she regained consciousness.

"Sweetheart," I said.

"Mom, what happened?" she whispered.

"Just too much smoke in your little lungs, honey. Don't worry, everything will be okay." The nurse pulled back the curtain and rolled a portable x-ray machine into the room. "I'll be just outside, Jaycee," I said. I walked down the hall looking for a water fountain. I was parched, and had that desperate feeling you get when thirst overcomes you. I spotted a lounge with a water fountain, several sofas, and a few tables and chairs scattered around. I quenched my thirst and sat down to think. What just happened? How did the fire start? Why were we trapped in the ladies room? Was someone trying to kill us, or was it some sort of bizarre accident? Did this have anything to do with the dealership, or Kopeck's barn?

As I waited for Jaycee to get x-rays, my thoughts drifted back to the conversation with Mike Smythe at the Willow Inn. If he recognized me from the days back in Philadelphia, he didn't let on. But what if he had recognized me? What if he got word that I was snooping around on Andy Gleason's behalf? What if he suspected that Andy thought he was somehow responsible for Danny's death? Did he think that I was trying to help Andy pin a murder rap on him?

Or maybe he was afraid that I knew too much about the Philadelphia Press embezzlement case and that I would blow his cover with the Wellington elite, or that I might even try to blackmail him. He may have suspected that Bart filled me in on the gory details of that scandal when we were married and he was representing Smythe.

Suddenly it occurred to me that Bart himself might be behind the fire that almost killed Jaycee and me. Bart is a scum bag, but I could never believe that he would put Jaycee in harm's way. He would had to have hired someone to set the fire since he was still in jail, and maybe the arsonist didn't know or care that Jaycee was in the ladies room with me. Or, maybe Bart might have coerced Smythe into setting the fire himself. Smythe might not have had the money to pay Bart's legal bills, and God help anyone who owed Bart Skeleton money and didn't pay up. Of course, there was the possibility that Smythe had nothing to do with it. Sloane Parker had told me that Bart was cellmates with that mobster, Ryan Adler. He could have gotten his mob connections to set that fire. They wouldn't care if Jaycee was killed, as long as they got me and Bart got his revenge.

None of this explained how or why Jaycee's Jungle Burger had been poisoned, if it had indeed been poisoned on purpose. I needed answers to these questions. Until then, Jaycee and I were in danger. I had to find out if Bart had anything to do with this, and my best bet was Sloane Parker. Sloane told me that she had connections at the Rockville State Penitentiary where Bart was incarcerated. I hoped that she would be able to find out if Bart had made contact with Smythe or anyone else on the outside who may have tried to kill me and Jaycee.

I pulled my cell phone out of my purse and hit Sloane's number.

"Hello Ivy! What a coincidence! I was just thinking about you, and I planned to call you later today."

I was surprised to hear her say that. "Really Sloane, what's up?"

"I heard from my contact at Rockville this morning. He told me that Ryan Adler was sent to solitary last week for pulling a shiv on one of the guards."

"Wow! Why did he do that?"

"I hear he's having a hard time taking orders, so they had to rough him up a little bit. Seems he tried to get his revenge. He's got a lot to learn about surviving in prison."

I thought about that momentarily. "What about Bart?"

"Bart's still on the cell block, and he's keeping a low profile. That's all I have on him" she said.

Given the circumstances, it wasn't conclusive one way or the other regarding Bart's involvement with the fire at Joe's. He could have set a plan in motion before Adler was sent to solitary—that's true. However, it would be much more difficult without Ryan's contacts. Even getting Smythe to do the dirty work would be tough, but with Bart you never knew. After explaining what happened to us at Joe's, I asked Sloane to keep her ear to the ground.

Sandy sat on the bench outside Joe's Bar and Grill sobbing into her apron. Tommy walked over and put his hand on her shoulder in an effort to comfort her. Fire Captain DeWeiss approached them. "Are you two okay?" he asked.

"Sure," Tommy said. Sandy looked anything but okay.

"Do you have any idea what happened?"

"No, I was scrubbing off the stove in the kitchen when Sandy came running in yelling fire! I ran into the bar and saw smoke coming out of the heating vents. All the old guys were running out the door. I looked around and I didn't see anybody else, then the fire alarm went off. Sandy and I both ran out of there and we were standing on the sidewalk waiting for you guys to show up, when I remembered about Jaycee and Ms. Snow. They were having lunch at table six. I thought about it, and I realized that I never brought them their check. I figured they must of ran out before Sandy came in to get me. I looked around, but I didn't see them. The smoke was getting really thick by then. They aren't the type to run off, so I figured they must still be in there somewhere. As soon as you guys got here, I said to go and look for them. How are they? Are they okay?" Tommy wanted to know.

"We don't know," DeWeiss said. Tommy shook his head back and forth in silence. By then, Sandy had regained her composure. She told DeWeiss that she had better call Joe and tell him what happened. She couldn't for the life of her remember where Joe was. Africa? New Zealand? The Canary Islands? Somewhere off shooting something. She breathed a heavy sigh and burst into tears again.

One of the firefighters came up to DeWeiss and pulled him aside. They spoke for a few minutes and then DeWeiss turned to Sandy and Tommy. "Do you know why anyone would deliberately want to set fire to this place?" Sandy looked up at Tommy and they both looked at DeWeiss.

"I don't," Tommy said.

Sandy squirmed, her eyes shifted left then right. "I don't know who did it, but I might know why."

DeWeiss nodded his head and prodded her on.

"We've been getting these notes lately," she said. "They're from some animal rights fanatics protesting against Joe's big-game hunting. They threatened to stop him no matter what it took. I told Joe we should call the police, but he didn't take them seriously. He put on his tough-guy attitude, and told me to ignore them."

"Do you have the notes?" DeWeiss asked.

"No" she said. "Joe probably threw them away."

"Do you know if Ivy Snow or her daughter were mixed up in any of this?"

"The animal-rights thing?" Sandy asked. "I don't think so, but I really don't know them that well."

DeWeiss walked around to the other side of the bench and sat down next to her. "My men tell me that when they got here that Tommy told them to go in and look for Ms. Snow and her kid. When they went into the back, they heard pounding coming from the bathroom door, and when they tried to open the door it wouldn't budge. Seems it was wedged shut from underneath."

Sandy stared at him in disbelief. "Thank God they're okay. They could have died in there."

DeWeiss's cell phone rang; it was the hospital.

"They think the mother will be all right—but they're not sure about the girl."

CHAPTER TWENTY

Tommy drove his beat-up 1998 red Ford Bronco down the long gravel road that led to the riding club. He figured he could probably find Ziggy there, since it was early morning and the stalls would need to be mucked out. Ziggy's job at the stable involved a lot of muck. Besides cleaning out 30 stalls a day, he had to sweep it out of the aisles and spread it over the field for fertilizer. The job paid minimum wage, but Ziggy didn't care. He got to look at all those pretty girls in their tight riding breeches and tall black leather boots. It more than made up for all the shit that he was knee-deep in.

Tommy parked the Bronco and went into the stable in search of Ziggy. He found him in the fifth stall, muck fork in hand, singing along to one of his favorite country songs, "Take This Job and Shove It."

"Hey!" Tommy shouted over the music.

Ziggy turned around and smiled at his cousin. "What brings you here, dude?"

"I want to talk to you, Ziggy. Did you hear about the fire at Joe's?"

"Yeah, I heard about it. Place didn't burn to the ground though, did it?"

"No, Ziggy, it didn't, but there was a lot of smoke

damage. Did you know that Ms. Snow and Jaycee got locked in the bathroom and almost suffocated?"

"No, I didn't hear about that," Ziggy said. "But it would've served them right. Especially that little bitch Jaycee. Tommy, you should've heard what she said about you on Facebook. She said that Tim Kopeck knows who burned down his barn, and that it was you. Everyone around here was talking about it."

Tommy froze. His mind was racing, trying to pull it all together. "What did you say, Zig? You know that I didn't burn down that barn."

"Yeah, but you were there," said Ziggy.

If Zig wasn't so damn stupid, and his blood relative, he would ditch him in a New York minute. But he was blood, and that was that. "Listen, Zig, I think it's time we got out of here for a while. Things aren't looking good, and if they try to stick the blame on anybody for those fires it'll be me. I just don't think we should hang around here anymore."

"Well, where would we go, Tommy? We don't know nobody any place else, and we ain't got no money," Ziggy whined.

"I've been thinking about that," said Tommy. "You remember Frank Giannetti?"

"Yeah, he was in your grade in school, wasn't he?"

"That's right, Zig. Well, Frank joined the Army and he's doing pretty well."

140

"The Army?" Ziggy scrunched up his face. "You think we should join the Army, Tommy?"

"Yeah, Zig, I do. We can get away from here, and we'll have everything we need."

"But what about my ma, Tommy? She'll be all alone."

Don't worry about that, Zig. My mom will look after her. They're sisters, remember?"

"Okay, Tommy, if you say so. What about Sandy?"

"I'm going to see her now. Finish your work and collect your pay. We'll say goodbye to the folks before we leave."

Tommy stood very close to Sandy. "Listen, baby, it won't be forever. After boot camp I'll send for you."

"Tommy, have you lost your mind? You can't go running off to the Army with me having a baby. You're running out on us—that's what you're doing!"

"No, Sandy, I'd never do that to you and the baby. I just got to get out of here till the heat dies down. You know they'll blame me for Kopeck's barn—and who knows what else."

"Tommy, I want to go with you."

"You know you can't join the Army, Sandy, you're

pregnant. Besides, Ziggy's coming with me. I don't want to leave him here. I'm afraid he'll shoot off his big mouth."

"That lowlife cousin of yours. If it wasn't for him you wouldn't be in this trouble."

"You know Ziggy's the kind that needs to be looked after, Sandy."

Her eyes brimmed with tears. Tommy moved closer and took her in his arms. He kissed her lightly on the lips, and then with passion and desperation. "I'll never leave you, Sandy. When this is over, we'll get married. I promise."

With that, his heavy boots clattered down the wooden porch steps. He slammed the door of his truck and took off—broken muffler roaring. Sandy stood, staring through the screen door, watching the sun set on her life.

CHAPTER TWENTY-ONE

Mike Smythe ambled out to the mailbox to see what came in that day. Ever since the onslaught of e-mail, there was never anything interesting. Junk mail and bills; it was hardly worth the trip. He pulled out five or six envelopes and quickly shuffled through them. The usual, except for this one pink envelope that had no postage stamp or return address. Curious, he wondered what it might be, and took it back into the house. He sat on his favorite velvet wing chair and gingerly opened the back flap. As he pulled out the contents, his heart nearly stopped. It was a Polaroid picture of him dressed in a black sequined evening gown leaving Morgan House. Every fiber in his body froze. His hands began to shake. Who did this? Who saw him? Who put this in his mailbox? If his friends found out he would be ruined, despised, ostracized. What about his kids? They would be mortified; they'd never speak to him again. A wave of panic shot through him. What could he do? He looked inside the envelope again and saw a piece of white paper folded in half. He removed it as if he were handling something toxic. There were letters cut out of magazines. The note said I KNOW ALL ABOUT YOU. I'LL BE IN TOUCH.

Mike felt a wave of nausea come over him.

Who could have put it in his mailbox? His mind raced, conjuring up anyone who could have a reason for doing such a thing. Was it someone from the past with a long-held grudge? Was it someone he saw every day? What do they want from him? No, it was that Ivy Snow. He was sure that what he had suspected about her all along was true. Bart Skeleton was right. Any doubts he had dissipated. She knew all about the embezzlement charge in Philadelphia, and she had been spying on him...obviously. Now she was putting her plan to blackmail him in motion. If only she hadn't escaped that fire at Joe's, none of this would be happening!

He was waiting for the other shoe to drop, and it was driving him mad with fear. He had to get out of the house; the walls were closing in on him. He got the keys to the car, and went around back to the garage. He slid in behind the wheel and turned on the ignition. He looked into the rearview mirror preparing to back out when something behind the visor caught his eye. It was a pink envelope. He gasped, and the adrenaline shot through his veins like hot molten lava. He could hardly bring himself to touch it, but he had to know. He tore open the envelope, and extracted the note.

Put $100,000 in a brown paper bag. Take it to Joe's bar at exactly 2:30 tomorrow afternoon. Leave it in the men's room. If you don't every member of the Field & Stream Club will get a copy of that picture.

What was he going to do? He didn't have
$100,000. He was afraid to go anywhere near the men's
room at Joe's. He couldn't go to the police. He needed a
drink. His hands were shaking as he tried to steady them
on the steering wheel. He backed the car out, took a deep
breath, and headed for the club. As he pulled into the
parking lot he spotted Melinda's car. What was she doing
here, he wondered. He sat quietly for a moment. An idea
came to him. He hurried into the club to find Melinda. She
was over at the front desk talking to the receptionist. He
tapped her on the shoulder. She spun her head around,
saw that it was Mike, and quickly collected herself. "Mike,
what a nice surprise!" she said with a broad smile on her
face. He returned a grin, and put his arm around her
shoulder. She was wearing cashmere again. This time a
pink formfitting sweater dress. It looked very
expensive—a good sign.

"Melinda, my dear, what brings you here? he
asked.

"Oh, I'm just dropping off a seating chart for this
month's DAR luncheon."

"Could I possibly persuade you to join me for a
cocktail?"

"Well, I think I have the time," she purred.

They went into the bar and sat at a remote table
in the corner. The waiter came over, and they both
ordered an Old-Fashioned. "You know, Melinda, I'm

really glad that I ran into you today. You've been on my mind quite a bit lately."

"Really?" she asked, "In what way?"

"I've just been thinking about how much your dear friendship means to me."

Melinda was slightly taken aback. Mike had never expressed his feelings for her before. What was coming? Could this mean…? Maybe he was ready to move their relationship to the next level. She licked her lips. "Well, of course I feel the same way about you, Mike," she said. Just then their drinks arrived, giving Mike much needed courage.

"Melinda, I feel that we've become so close over the past few months. It's comforting to know that I have someone whom I can truly rely on."

"Of course, Mike, you know you can always count on me."

"I'm relieved to hear that, my dear. I'm afraid that I have a little favor to ask of you."

Melinda was puzzled. Favor? What kind of favor did Mike want from her? It didn't sound like this was headed in the direction she was hoping for.

"You see, my dear, I seem to have found myself in an awkward situation," he said.

"What kind of situation?"

"Well, unfortunately, it's the kind of situation that requires me to come up with one-hundred thousand dollars by tomorrow."

Melinda's eyes flew open. "One-hundred thousand? What do you need a hundred thousand for?"

Mike stared into his low-ball glass and fidgeted with the swizzle stick. "I can't explain right now, but it's vitally important. You have to trust me, Melinda."

Wait a minute, she thought, isn't he supposed to be the rich guy? Why is he looking to me for money? "Mike, I don't understand. You are quite secure, are you not?"

"Melinda, it's very complicated. It would only be a loan. I'll pay you back—I promise," he pleaded.

Well, this is an unfortunate turn of events, she thought. "Mike, you know I would help you if I could," she lied. "But I can't get that kind of money by tomorrow."

Beads of sweat began to trickle onto his brow. "Do you know anyone who would lend me the money?" he asked in desperation. Melinda squirmed in her chair. She was getting angrier by the minute. Smythe was supposed to be her cash cow, and here he was asking her for money. She thought about Bertrand. He would be livid.

"Listen, Mike, I don't have the money, and I can't get the money. You have to find it somewhere else."

Humiliated, Mike felt nothing but despair. They finished their drinks in silence.

Melinda took her time getting back to her office.

147

She had no idea what she was going to do now. She entered the room and found Bertrand waiting for her. She spilled the story of her meeting with Mike, the words coming out of her mouth in a babble.

Bertrand landed a glancing blow across Melinda's jawbone that sent her reeling backward across the room into a bookcase. She put her hand up to her face in a protective gesture that came too late. "You stupid bitch," he said. "You told me that you could get the money. First you said that the insurance would pay out, and if not you could get it from Smythe. What am I supposed to do now?"

"Bertrand... Bertrand, I did everything I could, I promise you."

"They will hold me responsible. My life will be worth nothing."

Melinda thought fast. "It's not too late, we can still get the money."

"How?" he asked.

"Do you remember the large painting of a horse on the wall in Mike's living room?"

Bertrand thought back to his visit at Morgan House. He remembered seeing a number of paintings on the walls. Yes! The horse. Very fine.

"That painting is a Hobart," Melinda said. "It's worth a fortune. I'll call Mike and tell him that I want to take him out for a drink. I'll tell him I'm sorry I acted the way I did about the money, and I want to make it up to him. I'll offer to pick him up, and make sure that the doors are left unlocked when we leave. You can remove the painting from the wall, and we'll sell it on the black market."

Bertrand thought about the plan. It seemed fairly simple. He could not think of a reason why it would not work. If they could get enough for it maybe everything would be okay. "It's worth trying," he said. "We can do nothing else. When can it be done?"

"As soon as I can make the arrangements," Melinda said. "I'll call Mike right now."

CHAPTER TWENTY-TWO

I puttered around Little Paddocks cleaning tack, changing lightbulbs, filling water buckets, etc.: things that had to be done, no doubt. But I didn't kid myself. I was avoiding calling Andy. I knew I should get in touch with him and tell him about my talk with Smythe, but I knew he would be disappointed. Although I could put Smythe and Danny together at Joe's right before the fire, I couldn't put Smythe at the scene of the crime. Or for that matter, with a plausible motive for killing Danny Gleason other than sheer evil.

I went into the house and headed for the living room. It's my favorite room in the house. It has a massive stone fireplace that makes winters in the mountains bearable. I sat down on the burgundy leather chair next to the phone and picked up the heavy receiver. It was one of those reproduction black Bakelite phones like they used in the forties. A little indulgence that allowed me to choose style over cutting-edge technology. Of course I have an iPhone that I use almost constantly for work and keeping up with the kids. But Little Paddocks is one place in my life where I choose not to live at the speed of light. Andy picked up the phone on the second ring, as though he was expecting the call. "Hello Ivy, I was hoping it would be you."

"Hi, Andy. I thought I'd better give you a call and keep you up-to-date with what's going on."

"Did you find out anything about Smythe?" he asked.

"Not a lot, I'm afraid. I did verify that he was with your brother at Joe's right before the fire. Both Sandy and one of the customers saw them together. They said that he left in a huff, and that Danny seemed stunned, but neither of them overheard their conversation."

"It doesn't sound like things went very well, does it?" Andy asked.

"No, and neither of them thought much of Smythe. Oh! Here's a piece of news. Did you know that Smythe is dating your cousin Melinda?"

"What?" he blurted into the receiver. "No, I didn't know that. Are you sure?"

"I saw them together at the Field & Stream Club the other night, and she let me know in no uncertain terms that he is *off limits*."

"Wow, I wonder why she never said anything to me about it?"

"I don't know, maybe she was keeping it low key with the family," I said.

"Well, that's interesting, but I don't see what it could have to do with Danny's death."

"Me neither, but you never know. By the way,

there was one other thing that struck me as strange."

"What's that?" he asked.

"It seems as though Smythe has a job as a school bus driver."

"A school bus driver? You've got to be kidding. Why would a guy like Smythe drive a school bus? He's got big bucks, so he wouldn't need the money. He's always been a big shot in newspapers and politics. This doesn't fit the picture."

"I agree, Andy. The bus garage is just down the road from your dealership. I'll make an excuse to pay them a visit on my way into town. I'll see what I can find out."

"Please don't give up on this, Ivy." Andy's voice was shaky. "I know Smythe had something to do with Danny's death. I can't sleep at night, and I'm barely choking down my food. If I'm right about Smythe, I have a big score to settle."

"Take it easy, Andy. I'll let you know as soon as I learn more." I hung up the phone and a chill came over me. Andy was beginning to sound unhinged. Something told me that I didn't have any time to lose, so I put on a clean pair of jeans with a chambray shirt, jumped into the Z, and headed for the bus garage.

When I got there, I noticed a sign out front that said DRIVERS NEEDED. That gave me an idea. I walked through the front door; squeaky hinges made an eerie sound that echoed in the massive garage.

It was dim and dingy. The bus company must be trying to save on electric bills. The pungent smell of diesel fumes and engine grease assaulted my nostrils. I looked around, trying to find signs of life. Seeing no one, I called out. "Hey! Anybody here?"

To the right, a door slowly opened, spilling light into the garage. A woman poked her head out and yelled, "I'm in here."

I walked over and noticed a sign that said OFFICE painted on the frosted glass. I stepped inside a room suffocated in junk. Good grief, the place was a wreck. Files and folders piled up everywhere. Stacks of old newspapers, magazines and junk mail littered the place. The woman that called to me was back behind her desk, engulfed in paperwork. She was about 65. Her hair was permed into tight little curls and was dyed an impossible shade of red. I noticed a name tag pinned to her royal blue fleece vest. It told me her name was Midge.

"What can I do for you?" she asked.

I made up a story about my brother moving to the area and looking for a job. I told her that an old friend, Mike Smythe, suggested he apply here.

"Your brother is a friend of Mike Smythe?" she asked.

"Yes, they knew each other way back when they both lived in Philadelphia. Mike does work here, doesn't he?

"Part-time," Midge said. "He fills in for drivers who are sick or on vacation."

"Knowing Mike, driving a bus is kind of an odd thing for him to be doing, don't you think, Midge?"

"Yes, I suppose so, but he said that he does it because he simply adores kids."

Mike Smythe adores kids? Somehow that idea just didn't fit the picture. I thanked Midge for her help and assured her that my "brother" would be in touch. I needed to think all of this over and decide on my next move. A cup of tea was in order.

I sat alone in the Perk Me Up Café sipping green tea and munching on one of their homemade scones, which are said to be the best this side of Scotland. Having never been to Scotland I really couldn't make that call, but they are delicious. I had all these pieces of a puzzle, but I was struggling to put them together. Melinda kept popping up everywhere in this ordeal. Related to Danny and Andy, dating Smythe, having a fling with Bertrand. For an environmental consultant she sure got around. I couldn't stop thinking about Jaycee's vision of Melinda and Bertrand holding hands by the banks of a river, with the heady perfume of lavender in the air. What did it mean?

I was so busy with all of this, I had not been keeping very close tabs on Bertrand. His research on the polo industry was finished, so I got him started researching for an article on dressage. It was a lot of work, but it still left him time for extracurricular activities. Just then, Roberta Bristol walked through the door. She was wearing a rose-colored knit tracksuit and yellow Keds. "Hi, Roberta," I said, smiling.

"Hello, Ivy. Don't you look cozy sitting there with your afternoon tea and scones?"

"I'm feeling sort of British today," I said in a terrible fake accent. "Won't you join me?" She sat down at the table and told the waitress that she would have what I was having. "So what's new with you, Roberta? How are things at the Coach House?"

"It's going along pretty well. I had a group of Algerian tourists in last week. They spoke French, so they yakked it up with Bertrand, sometimes till the wee hours. Too bad I couldn't understand a word they said."

"Funny, Bertrand didn't say anything to me about it."

"Well, he might not," said Roberta. "He keeps things pretty close to the vest."

I'll say he does, I thought. Especially his office amore. "Roberta, do you ever see Bertrand going out with anyone, you know, like on a date?"

"No, I haven't, and it surprises me. He is sort of full of himself, you know. Thinks he's hot stuff. I do hear him Skyping someone for hours late at night, though, and

I think it's a woman. I can't make out the voices real good, but I'd bet on it. What guy would spend that much time Skyping another guy unless it was some sort of big business deal, or he was, as they say, a little light in the loafers?" She giggled.

"I don't know, but Skype is worldwide, so could be anyone."

"I guess. You know, for someone so private, he does ask a lot of questions."

"Questions about what, Roberta?"

"Oh, everything. He always wants to know how we do this and that over here. Why anyone would want to talk about sewers and septic systems, for instance, is beyond me. Maybe it has something to do with the sewers of Paris. Maybe he has a Phantom of the Opera fixation? Who knows?" She took a big gulp of her tea. "Listen, Ivy, I've got to be going. I have people checking in at four thirty and I don't want to be late."

"Sure, Roberta, nice seeing you," I said.

Interesting. I reviewed the facts, and for the first time, it hit me. Melinda was out of the country at the same time that Bertrand was applying for his internship. As a matter of fact, she traveled to Europe quite a bit. I wondered how the environmental situation was in France.

I picked up my phone and pressed the button that would connect me to Crystal.

"Hi, Ivy! I was just about to call you."

"Really? What's going on?"

"I have a showing with Melinda tomorrow—the Crawford place. Thought I'd let you know in case you wanted me to do any sleuthing."

"Well, as a matter of fact, there is some information that I'd like you to get."

"What's that?" Crystal asked.

"I have a feeling that there is more to Melinda's relationship with Bertrand than huggy-kissy."

"What do you mean?"

"I think there's a good chance that Melinda knew Bertrand before he ever came to Wellington."

"You're kidding? What makes you think that?"

"It all started with a vision that Jaycee has been having. She keeps seeing Bertrand and Melinda holding hands near a river, with the scent of lavender in the air. She sees many bridges, and a pink aura surrounding them."

"Weird."

"I'm beginning to think that Bertrand's internship from the Sorbonne in Paris isn't a coincidence. I think it might be part of something bigger."

"Like what?" Crystal asked.

"Like I don't know," I said. "That's what I'd like you to find out if you can."

"I'll do my best. Gotta go, Ivy."

I hung up the phone and headed home to Little Paddocks.

CHAPTER TWENTY-THREE

Crystal pulled her dark blue Jeep Cherokee into Melinda's driveway at ten sharp. She knew how Melinda hated to be kept waiting, and being with her was difficult enough when she wasn't angry. The garage door began to open slowly, and before her eyes appeared a big black Mercedes sedan with Melinda behind the wheel. She gestured for Crystal to come over.

"We're taking my car," Melinda announced.

"Really, I don't mind driving."

"It's not that. I get edgy when other people drive. I like to be in control."

Crystal climbed into the passenger seat and buckled her seatbelt. Melinda whipped around the Cherokee, and turned into Hickory Lane. She knew her way to the Crawford place—she'd been to enough parties there. Poor David and Hillary Crawford. My, how the mighty had fallen. They thought they were "all that" with their over-the-top dinner parties, moonlight buffets, and Hunt Breakfasts. They always had to outdo everyone else. Those union workers finally brought them to their knees. Now they were getting their comeuppance. Hillary would die if she knew I was looking at their house, Melinda thought.. And look I will—every nook and cranny.

"Crystal, have you any buyers for my house lined up?"

"Ah, yes, as a matter of fact I do. There is a couple who is being transferred to the United States from Paris. They are anxious to see your house." Crystal shot a sideways glance at Melinda.

Melinda's smile froze. "Paris? Who on earth would be transferred from Paris, France, to Wellington, Pennsylvania?"

"What do you mean?" Crystal fought back an urge to chuckle.

"I think it's kind of unusual, don't you?"

"Not really. After all, Bertrand came here from Paris."

Melinda's antenna went up. She felt she was somehow on shaky ground here. She didn't want to discuss Bertrand with Crystal. She didn't like where this conversation was going—at all. "Are there any other potential buyers?"

"Not at the moment," Crystal said.

They reached the Crawford place. David and Hillary were in New York, so Crystal used the lockbox. They walked into the foyer and were immediately bathed in sunlight that streamed down through the skylights in the thirty-foot ceilings. When they bought the farmhouse, the Crawfords brought in Nathaniel Deeds, one of the country's foremost architects, who had the entire place gutted and remodeled.

"Lovely, isn't it?" asked Crystal.

"Well, it's bright enough. I'll have to wear sunglasses in the house," Melinda quipped.

Crystal mentally rolled her eyes. As they walked through the house, Melinda examined every inch. Suddenly, she announced her intention to use the powder room. She ducked inside and closed the door, but Crystal hovered nearby. Melinda whipped out her cell phone and called Bertrand. Their entire conversation was in French.

"Listen, baby, we have a big problem," Melinda started out.

"What do you mean?" Bertrand said impatiently.

"That nosy bitch Crystal Prichard is up to something. She's deliberately baiting me, saying that she's showing my house to a couple from Paris. I know it's a lie, but she's trying to get a reaction out of me."

"You are being paranoid."

"No, no. She thinks she's being subtle, clever, but I see right through her. She even had the nerve to bring your name into the conversation,"

Bertrand was silent for a moment. "What did she say about me?"

"Nothing incriminating, but you are on her radar screen."

"You better get rid of her, Melinda. I told you it

was a crazy idea to hire her in hope of getting dirt on Ivy Snow."

"It's not a crazy idea. She already spilled the beans about Ivy's ex-husband. I've been in touch with Bart Skeleton at Rockville state prison. He's going to come in real handy, and soon."

"Nothing will be worth it if we don't get that money, *mon cheri*."

"I know darling, we will."

"Have you talked to Smythe?"

"Yes. Everything is set up for tonight. Must go now, darling, goodbye." She pressed the end call button, opened the door, and peered out into the hallway. No sign of Crystal.

Crystal had concealed herself behind Hillary Crawford's armoire, and heard every word of Melinda's conversation with Bertrand. Fortunately, French was her best subject in school, so she understood every word that Melinda had said. She was shocked to learn that Melinda was communicating with Bart in prison. The question was, why? She bristled at the thought that she had let the cat out of the bag about Bart. This couldn't be good news for Ivy. And what about this money that they are trying to get their hands on? What's it for? How did Mike Smythe fit into all of this? A lot of unanswered questions. She had her work cut out for her.

Melinda finished the tour of the Crawford house,

and informed Crystal that it would not be suitable. The rooms were too small, and the quality of the construction was not up to par. Crystal sighed deeply and climbed back into the passenger seat of Melinda's Mercedes.

CHAPTER TWENTY-FOUR

It was already very late, but I was still at the office finishing up my work for the day and trying to make sense of the craziness going on around me. We were running behind schedule on every project. I wondered if Bertrand had finished the dressage research. I headed over to his desk to see where he stood, but Bertrand wasn't there. Although I told myself that I had to keep a close eye on him, I just wasn't able to. I had to be there for Jaycee, who was finally herself again after the fire at Joe's.

Between keeping up with business and trying to help Andy, Bertrand had definitely slipped through the cracks. I walked around to the other side of his desk, and opened his laptop. The dressage research was not on the screen. Instead, I was shocked to see the Al Jazeera website. It was all in Arabic, so I had no idea what it said. I didn't know that Bertrand could speak Arabic; he didn't note that skill on his résumé. Whatever was going on here wasn't good. I distrusted Bertrand from the day we met, but up until now his actions seemed innocent enough. And what about Melinda and her unlikely relationship with Bertrand? Jaycee had that vision about them. Something was going on and it was about time I got some answers.

I locked the door to the office and headed for East Main Street in search of Bertrand. By now it was getting dark outside, and I was grateful for the carriage lamps that lighted the Commons. As I approached Morgan House, I saw Mike's car shoot out of the driveway and speed away downhill. Where was he going? Why was he driving so fast? I looked toward the house and saw that the door was standing wide open. Why would Mike leave the door open? Was he that careless? I climbed the few stone steps to the porch and entered the living room. "Oh my God," I gasped. Mike was lying in the middle of the floor covered in blood.

I jumped back momentarily and grabbed onto the door frame to steady myself. Was he dead? I rushed over to his side and clenched my hand around his wrist, feeling for a pulse. Nothing. I noticed a long brass tubular object covered in blood next to his head. I looked up through the kitchen door to see yellow flames dancing around the room. The house was on fire! I had to get out of there! I had to get Mike out of there in case he was still alive.

I decided to try dragging him out the front door, so I grabbed him under the arms and tried to lift his heavy body. He weighed a ton. I'd never be able to get him out the door. What was I going to do? Panic began to flood my brain. I couldn't budge him, but I couldn't leave him there either. I could feel perspiration running down my face as the heat from the fire became more intense. Smoke was billowing out into the living room, and the pungent odor seared the delicate membranes in my nose. I could not let my pyrophobia get the best of me now! I tugged again, hoping that I could drag his immense body to the door. It was no use.

Suddenly I felt a hand on my shoulder. I spun my head around to see Officer Stuart of the Wellington police standing over me. He took my arm and pulled me through the door into the fresh night air, then ran back into the house and dragged Mike out just as an ambulance arrived. Within seconds I could hear the sirens of the Township fire trucks as they came flying toward Morgan House. I was afraid it was too late. The house was engulfed in flames.

Roberta came up behind me wrapped in her pink fleece robe, arms flailing in the air like a giant pterodactyl. The Coach House was perilously close to the fire. If just one cinder flew onto her roof it could mean disaster. "Where is Mike Smythe?" she screeched. Officer Stuart came over to her and put a blanket around her shoulders.

"Mrs. Bristol, I'm afraid Mr. Smythe is dead," he said.

We all looked at each other, unable to speak at the sheer horror of it all. Just then, John Garrett pulled up in his black unmarked Dodge Charger. "Ivy, are you okay?" he said frantically

"Yes, I think so, John. I'm so glad to see you." I fought back my tears.

"What are you doing here, Ivy?"

"I just found Mike Smythe's body."

Garrett took in a deep breath, letting it out with a sigh. He shook his head back and forth in disbelief. This was going to be a nightmare. He gave Officer Stuart orders to manage the crime scene, and gently steered me toward his car. "We'd better go back to headquarters and you can tell me the whole story."

I texted Jayson to let him know I'd be late, and also asked him to keep a close eye on his sister. I dreaded leaving her alone after what happened at Joe's. He texted back not to worry.

We reached the station, and John ushered me into a miniscule room furnished with a folding table and two chairs. The police spared every expense on decorating unless you counted the large mirror that covered one wall. Being a mystery fan, it was not lost on me that this was the ubiquitous two-way mirror essential to any interrogation scene. He gestured for me to take a seat opposite the mirror, and he sat down across from me. I could see my reflection in that mirror and I looked awful. I suppose it was to be expected. I just found a dead body in a burning building. My chances of coming out looking like Sarah Jessica Parker were slim and none. I resigned myself to accept reality and waited to get the questioning over with. I saw that there was a tape recorder on the table. John hit the button, and began with the customary name, rank, and serial number. I then recounted the details of what had happened at Morgan House. I suddenly felt exhausted. It was like the adrenalin that kept me going so far had suddenly leaked out of my body.

"Ivy, how long have you known Mike Smythe?" asked Garrett.

"Not long," I replied. Even though it was John, I didn't like the idea of answering police questions in too much detail, especially without a lawyer present. After all, this was official business.

"Well, could you give me a vague idea?"

"I guess I met him about a week or so ago. He gave me that *go on* look. "I met him at the Field & Stream Club."

"How did the meeting come about?" he asked.

"I was there for dinner with Crystal. As we were being shown to our table, I spotted Melinda, a woman who sublets office space from me. She was having dinner with Smythe. We went over to say hello, and she introduced us."

"Who is this Melinda?" Garrett wanted to know.

I gave him her full name.

"Did you see Smythe after that?"

"Yes, as a matter of fact we had drinks at the Willow Inn a few nights later." I thought it might be in my best interest to elaborate at this point. "I knew Smythe was an antiques connoisseur and I wanted to recruit him to be on my auction fundraiser committee."

"Did he accept?" Garrett asked.

"Yes, he said he would be delighted to help. That's the last I saw of him."

"I see, and what brought you to Morgan House tonight?"

"Actually, I was there by accident. I was on my way to the Coach House looking for the intern that has been working for me at *Equine Style*. He's not from this country, so he's staying at the Coach House while he's in the U.S."

"And what is his name?"

"Bertrand Reynard. He's originally from Côte d' Ivoire, Africa, but he came here from Paris where he is studying at the Sorbonne."

Garrett made a note to ask Roberta Bristol about Bertrand Reynard, and turned off the tape recorder.

"Ivy, this has been a terrible experience for you. I want you to go home, have a nice hot cup of tea, and go to bed. I'll call you in the morning."

He drove me back to the parking lot where I had left the Z. I put the convertible top down. It was late, and a little chilly, but I needed the fresh air. On the way back to Little Paddocks, I reviewed the interrogation in my mind Oh! I just remembered something. John asked me how I first met Smythe. I told him about that evening at the Field & Stream Club, but I totally neglected to tell him about the past association in Philadelphia through Bart. Maybe I should have told him about the embezzlement charges at the Press, and that he had retained my ex-husband to defend him. That would be opening up a real can of worms. I needed to think this over very carefully.

Perhaps it would be best to tell John about the embezzlement charge, especially seeing as how there was an outside chance that Smythe was somehow involved with the fire at Joe's. It's not impossible to think that Bart put him up to it. But then again, if that were true it would give me a motive for getting rid of Smythe, and I was not about to cast suspicion on myself. There would be plenty of people in this town who would be just fine with that given that I'm a newcomer, and not a native Wellingtonian. After all, I was found leaning over his dead body. Much could be made of it. I had to find out who killed Smythe before they got around to blaming me. Where should I start? Maybe it was time to pay a visit to Andy Gleason.

CHAPTER TWENTY-FIVE

On my way into the office the next morning I stopped by the GM dealership hoping to catch Andy in. Even though he was part-owner of the business, he wasn't, as he said, a *suit*. He felt more comfortable in overalls and work boots, which was just as well since he oversaw the parts and repair departments. His office was located on the lower level so that he could be close to the action. I opened the heavy steel outer door and stepped into the garage. Several mechanics were hard at work in their bays. At least that part of the business was doing okay. "Hi guys," I said. "Is Andy around?" Jesse stuck out his thumb and motioned toward Andy's office. I knocked on his door, and heard, "Come in." I opened the door and stuck my head inside.

"Good morning, Andy." He swiveled his chair around to face me and I could tell he was startled.

"Ivy, I wasn't expecting you," he said.

"I know, but I thought I'd better stop by and tell you the news myself—before you heard from anyone else."

"What news?"

"Mike Smythe died last night."

Andy was silent for a moment or two. I watched

his face for reaction.

"How did it happen?

"It happened in a fire at his home, Morgan House."

"That's quite a shocker, but it's kind of ironic. Smythe dying in a fire, you know?" I knew exactly what Andy was thinking. "Was the fire an accident?" he asked.

"No, it wasn't an accident."

"How do you know?"

"Because I found the body."

"*You* found the body?" I could see the wheels turning in his head. "What were you doing at Morgan House?"

"I was on my way to the Coach House looking for Bertrand, and when I passed by Morgan House I noticed that the front door was standing wide open. I saw Mike's Smythe's car speeding down the hill, tires screeching. I went in to investigate and saw Mike lying on the floor in a pool of blood. He was beaten to a pulp. I tried to find his pulse to see if he was still alive, but I couldn't." For some reason, I held back mentioning the long brass tube that I found lying next to Mike's body.

"You're sure he was dead?" Andy asked.

I felt as though I was being interrogated. "No, I wasn't really sure, so when I saw the flames in the kitchen I tried to drag him out. The firemen got there just then, thank God."

"So, Smythe was murdered? Who do you think did it?"

"I don't know," I said. "There are numerous possibilities."

Andy sat in his office thinking things over for a very long time. Maybe if he had gone with Danny to ask Smythe for the money things would be different. It didn't really matter now. Smythe was dead, as he deserved to be, but it still didn't bring Danny back. That damn insurance company declared Danny's death a suicide anyway, so there would be no money to save the dealership, and no money to support Danny's wife and kids. He had failed everyone. He was the loser that he always believed himself to be.

He reached into the bottom drawer of his desk and pulled out a box of pink envelopes. They had served their purpose, so he threw the remainder in the wastebasket. He closed up the dealership and climbed into his Tahoe. He took the back way to Ravens Nest Road and parked on the ridge overlooking the town of Wellington.

The radio was playing the Johnny Cash classic "Burning Ring of Fire." Andy reached across the seat and opened the glove compartment. He drew out his Luger, put the barrel in his mouth, and pulled the trigger.

CHAPTER TWENTY-SIX

As soon as I walked into the building I knew something was up. My entire staff was crowded into Melinda's office, and spilling out into the hallway. I went over and pushed my way in. Melinda was sitting at her desk, crying hysterically, while the staff tried to comfort her. "What's going on?" I asked. Melinda shot a venomous look my way. "Mike Smythe is dead. That's what's going on," she hissed.

"Yes, Melinda, I know. I'm very sorry."

"*You*... sorry?"

I could see that this was going to escalate, so I thanked my staff and asked them to please get back to work. I shut the door so that Melinda and I could be alone.

"Yes, Melinda, I'm sorry about Mike. I know that the two of you were close."

"Do you now? I gather that you know a lot about Mike," she said sarcastically. "Since you were the one who found his body. Yes, I found out about that! What were you doing at Mike's place anyway?"

"It was just a coincidence. I was on my way to the Coach House looking for Bertrand. Bertrand! With all the horrible events of last night, I completely forgot about

Bertrand. He wasn't here with the rest of the staff. Where was he? I recalled the whole story to Melinda, but I could tell she didn't believe a word of it.

"Ivy, I know that you've been asking questions about Mike all over town," she said.

"Well, that's certainly an exaggeration. I was considering asking him to join my antiques auction committee, and I wanted to learn more about him, that's all."

"Liar!" she shouted, as she sprang up from her chair. "You wanted Mike Smythe for yourself."

I couldn't help it—I burst out laughing, which made her even angrier. "I don't see why you should care so much, Melinda, since you were doing Bertrand on the side."

"Doing Bertrand! You're crazy!" she shouted.

"Melinda, I saw the two of you together."

The color drained from her face. She thought about it for a moment, and then she smiled sweetly. "Well, Ivy, I guess you got me. Guilty as charged. She walked around to the front of her desk and perched herself on the edge. She was wearing a simple black sheath. Melinda almost never wore black; she said that it didn't flatter her skin tone. But she chose to wear it today, almost as if she were in mourning. Of course that couldn't be, since she only learned of Mike's death after she reached the office.

"Ivy, you have to admit that Bertrand is an attractive guy, and I've never been able to resist a French accent."

I thought about Jaycee's vision, and I decided to cast a line and see if she'd bite. "I know what you mean, Melinda. You're so lucky to be able to spend so much time in Paris with your job."

"I know. I practically live for those trips."

"How long has it been since you were there last?" I asked.

"Oh, back in the fall," she lamented.

That was about the time that Bertrand first contacted me about the internship. This was getting interesting. "How did you happen to meet Bertrand in Paris?"

"Well, we were..." Melinda's hand flew up to her mouth, clamping it shut. She jumped down off the desk. "What do you mean, Ivy?"

"Come on, Melinda, I know that you met Bertrand while you were in Paris last fall, and I know it was you who told him about my magazine. You wanted to get him over here to the States, so you suggested that he apply for an internship." Melinda glared at me. "I want to know what he's up to. He's here for more than a PhD dissertation and you know it. You've gotten yourself mixed up in whatever he's doing, and maybe you got Mike mixed up in it too!"

"I don't know what you're talking about, Ivy. I think you're just trying to divert attention away from the fact that you were found with Mike's dead body."

"Are you accusing me of murder, Melinda?"

"Not specifically. Not yet anyway, but I don't believe that you just happened to be at Morgan House last night."

"Believe what you want, but right now I just want to know where Bertrand is."

"I haven't the slightest idea."

"And you wouldn't tell me if you did," I said.

"No. Now please leave my office."

I turned to walk out, but not before noticing that she had bitten her fingernails down to the quick, on otherwise perfectly manicured hands.

As soon as her office door closed, Melinda picked up a leather-bound notebook on her desk and flung it across the room. Damn that Ivy Snow, she poked her nose into everything! Melinda paced back and forth, becoming more agitated by the minute. Where was Bertrand... *where?* She had been desperately trying to reach him on his cell phone all last night and all this morning. He either turned it off or the battery died. She knew nothing of what happened last night and she was sick with worry. Did he get the painting before Mike got home? Did he even make it to Morgan House as planned? Or, God forbid, did Mike catch him in act of stealing it?

Melinda hated the idea of calling Roberta Bristol at the Coach House, but it looked like she didn't have a choice. That woman was such a gossip. If she didn't know where Bertrand was she would certainly let the whole town know that Melinda was looking for him. No use putting it off. She picked up the receiver and punched in the number. Roberta answered the phone with her most welcoming innkeeper tone. "The Coach House, Roberta Bristol speaking, how may I help you?"

"Hi Roberta, it's Melinda calling." She tried to keep her voice as calm and steady as possible.

"What can I do for you?" The welcoming tone was gone.

"I was wondering if you might know where Bertrand is. His cell phone doesn't seem to be working."

"No, I don't know where Bertrand is. I haven't seen him since yesterday afternoon. He didn't come home last night," Roberta said. "What did you need to talk to him about? If he shows up, I can give him a message."

"Oh, never mind. I'm sure he'll be in touch sooner or later," Melinda said, trying to sound nonchalant. "Thanks anyway, Roberta." Melinda put down the receiver. Bertrand did not return to the Coach House last night. Ivy had been looking for him since late yesterday afternoon. Where was he? A feeling of cold fear crept throughout her body. What if Bertrand took off? What if he stole the Hobart and ran? The thought was so disturbing to Melinda that she couldn't completely form it in her mind. He would never do that to me, he loves me. He said that he wanted me by his side always; whatever had to be done, we would do it together. No, it's impossible. Perhaps there's been an accident; perhaps he's lying alone in a hospital bed somewhere, injured and frightened. I need to help him, she thought. Melinda opened her desk drawer and pulled out the local phone book. She turned to *H* for hospitals.

CHAPTER TWENTY-SEVEN

Detective Garrett sat at his desk trying to make sense out of what happened at Morgan House. The place was burned to the ground, so there wasn't a lot to learn there. Mrs. Bristol did tell him that Smythe owned a green vintage Cadillac Eldorado, and that it was missing. He had to find out what Smythe was doing and who he was with before the murder. He had no leads, so he decided to pay another visit to the Coach House. Maybe now that Mrs. Bristol had a chance to recover she might be able to tell him more.

He drove over to East Main Street and rang Roberta's doorbell. She answered it wearing dark denim "mom jeans" and a pink sweatshirt with green and purple smiling frogs all over the front. "Good morning, Mrs. Bristol," Garrett said. "How are you doing this morning?"

"Well, detective, I couldn't sleep at all last night, so I feel frazzled."

"Can't blame you for that," he said. "Mrs. Bristol, I'd like to ask you a few questions about your neighbor, Mr. Michael Smythe."

"Of course, Detective, come in." Good! Roberta was finally going to let people know what kind of a creep Mike Smythe was. "Would you like some coffee or tea,

Detective?" Roberta asked, always the consummate hostess. Garrett said he would prefer coffee, black, thank you very much. It only took a moment for Roberta to return from the kitchen, carrying a tray set with two coffee cups and a plate of her special chocolate chip cookies. She always kept a fresh pot of coffee brewing for her guests.

"Mrs. Bristol, what can you tell me about Mike Smythe?"

Roberta settled into her green and white plaid chair. "Well, Detective, he moved into Morgan House about five years ago, after he retired from the newspaper in Philadelphia. He was very small-minded... a very critical man." Roberta thought back to their ongoing battle over paint colors.

Did he have many friends?" Garrett asked.

"I didn't know his friends, but he belonged to the Field & Stream Club, and hung around with that crowd." Detective Garrett took notes. "He also tried to befriend that young African man who is staying here while he's doing an internship at *Equine Style*."

"What's his name?" Garrett asked.

"Bertrand Reynard. He came here from Paris a few weeks ago. He's studying at the Sorbonne, and working on his doctoral dissertation."

"How do you know that Smythe was trying to get friendly?"

"Bertrand told me," Roberta said. "One afternoon, Mike Smythe invited Bertrand into his house for a drink. Bertrand accepted, but he told me that Mike made him feel uncomfortable."

"Do you know in what way?"

"Detective Garrett, Mike Smythe could make anyone feel uncomfortable about anything. He was a snob, and very condescending."

Garrett studied Roberta. Obviously, she was no fan of Mike Smythe. "What about women, Mrs. Bristol? To your knowledge, did Smythe have a girlfriend? Was he dating anyone?"

"I don't know for sure," Roberta replied. "However, I have seen him with that Melinda what's her name… the one that shares an office with Ivy Snow."

"When was the last time you saw them together?"

"As a matter of fact, it was late yesterday afternoon. I saw them leaving Morgan House and they looked pretty chummy." Roberta started to speak again, but she hesitated. Should she tell this cop about seeing Mike Smythe in drag? Smythe was either gay, AC/DC, or a transvestite. She didn't know much about that kind of stuff. Could it have anything to do with his murder? It probably could. Maybe one of his cross-dressing friends killed him, who knew? I'd better tell. If he finds out about it and suspects that I knew and didn't tell him, he might think I was trying to hide something. "Detective Garrett, there is something you should know about Mike Smythe."

"What's that, Mrs. Bristol?"

"He liked to dress up in women's clothing."

Garrett just stared at Roberta. "How do you know?"

"I saw him with my own two eyes. He was leaving Morgan House dressed in a black sequined Yves Saint Laurent evening gown."

"Are you sure?"

"Of course I'm sure. I thought he was going to fall off the steps in his spike-heeled Jimmy Choos."

"Have you told anyone else about this?"

Roberta hesitated. "Well, I may have told one or two people. I really don't remember," Roberta lied.

"Mrs. Bristol, do you know any one person in particular who might have wanted Mike Smythe dead?"

Roberta rolled her eyes and lifted her shoulders in query. "Here, Detective, here's the phone book, start at the beginning."

Garrett smirked. "One more thing. Would it be possible for me to speak with Bertrand Reynard?"

"That I can't tell you," Roberta said. "I haven't seen him since yesterday morning. He didn't come home last night. You might want to ask that Melinda. She called here earlier today looking for him, maybe she's found him by now."

I decided to bring Jaycee into the office with me until the murderer was caught. She could do her cyber classes there, so that would keep her busy. Jayson was on the Appalachian Trail with his scout troop so I didn't have to worry about him, at least for the time being. I sat down at my desk and began downloading my e-mail when Garrett knocked on my door. "Come in, John, have a seat. Do you have any news?" I asked.

"Yes," he sighed. I learned that this Melinda woman that works here was with Smythe the evening of the murder. I'm here to see her, but I wanted to talk to you first."

"Well, John, let me clear something up. Melinda does not work for me; she simply sublets office space in this building."

"Okay then, do you know who she does work for?"

"Some foreign-based environmental company—I don't know which one. She's a consultant."

"I take it you two are not very close?"

"No, Detective, we are not!" I said with emphasis.

"Have you heard from Bertrand Reynard?"

"No. I haven't been able to get in touch with him. Frankly, I'm beginning to get worried. He doesn't know many people here and he doesn't have a car. He's not answering his cell phone and he's not at the Coach House; I checked with Roberta earlier."

"I just had a talk with Mrs. Bristol. She told me that Melinda called her this morning looking for Reynard."

"That doesn't surprise me," I said. "Melinda and Bertrand have a *thing* going on."

"Really? I thought that she and Smythe were together."

"I guess Melinda has a very complicated love life." I smiled.

"I think it's time I had a talk with her," Garrett said.

"She's down the hall, second door on the left."

Melinda was startled to see a complete stranger at her door. Garrett introduced himself and produced his badge. She invited him to sit in the desk chair opposite her.

"I'm here investigating the murder of Michael Smythe," he told her.

Melinda's eyes welled up with tears. "He was such a lovely man."

"What was your relationship with Smythe?"

"We were good friends, Detective. I knew Mike for a number of years." Melinda reached for a tissue and dabbed at her eyes.

"Friends," Garrett said. "Just friends, or was there more to it than that?"

"Just friends, Detective." Melinda wasn't going to give him any more information than she had to.

"When was the last time you saw Mike Smythe?"

She figured she'd better tell the truth about that, since a number of people had seen them together. "It was early yesterday evening. We went to the Willow Inn for drinks."

"How long were you two together?"

"Oh, just an hour or so. I dropped him off at his house and then went home myself." Melinda struggled to keep her voice steady.

"Is there anyone that can substantiate that?"

"No, I live alone," she said.

"What about Bertrand Reynard? Are you friends with him too?"

Garrett was getting intense. Melinda thought it best to put some distance between her and Bertrand.

"No," she said. "He just works in this office for Ivy Snow."

"Well, could you explain to me why you were looking for him this morning?"

Damn that Roberta Bristol and her big mouth. She knew she shouldn't have called her. She had to think fast to come up with a story. "Oh, yes. I wanted to ask him to return a book that I lent him."

"What book was that?" Garrett asked.

"*A Brief History of Time*," by Stephen Hawking." Melinda assumed that this lowbrow detective would know nothing of it.

"Great book," Garrett said. "I read it about fifteen years ago. I especially like the part about the dinosaurs, didn't you?"

"Yes… very interesting." Melinda was hoping that he wouldn't ask any more questions about the book, since she herself had not read it.

"Well, did you find him?"

"Find who, Detective?"

"Bertrand Reynard."

"No, I did not."

"When was the last time you saw him?"

"To be honest, I really don't remember. I don't keep tabs on him, you know."

Garrett walked out of Melinda's office and stopped in the hall to make a few notes. Let's see—she lied about Reynard and Hawking's book. She's probably lying about Smythe, too. I've got to keep a close eye on this one.

Garrett was about to leave the offices when he heard the sound of someone sobbing.

CHAPTER TWENTY-EIGHT

John hurried down the hall and found me holding Jaycee in my arms. She was shaking, and I stroked her hair trying to comfort her.

"What's going on?" he asked.

"John, this is my daughter, Jaycee." Jaycee turned her head slightly to have a look at Garrett.

"What's the matter with her?"

"Let's go to my office, where we can have some privacy. We proceeded to my office, and before closing the door I checked the hallway to make sure no one was lurking about. "John, Jaycee has been trying to tell me something that may have a bearing on the Smythe murder case."

"Really?" He looked surprised. "What do you know, Jaycee?"

Jaycee looked at him dubiously. Then she looked at me. I ran interference. "John, there is something you need to know. It might not be easy to understand at first, but my daughter has extrasensory perception."

Garrett raised his brow. He had never actually met anyone with ESP, but he knew that law enforcement worked with such "consultants" from time to time. He wasn't sure if he believed it was real. "How do you know?" he asked.

"She's had premonitions and visions ever since she was a little girl. We had her tested at the Chautauqua Institute and they confirmed what we suspected all along. She actually does have ESP." Garrett sat quietly, trying to let it sink in. "Jaycee is trying to tell me about a vision that she just had—it frightened her badly. "Jaycee, honey, tell Detective Garrett about your vision. Start at the beginning."

Jaycee was reluctant, but she spoke." I had a vision about a fire. There was this big fire, and there were two soldiers standing there watching it. The flames were shooting up high into the air, and at first I couldn't tell what was burning. But then I did see. It was a big green car. It was kind of old-fashioned looking. The soldiers just kept watching as the fire grew. There was something familiar about them. As my vision got clearer I could see their faces, and I knew them. It was Ziggy, the stable hand at the riding club, and Tommy, the waiter from Joe's. As the fire got hotter and hotter, their skin started melting off their bodies. It was horrible." Jaycee buried her head in her hands. I put my arm around her and pulled her close to me. I looked at John and I could tell that he was debating with himself whether or not to believe Jaycee.

"Ivy," he said, "this might have something to do with the Smythe case."

"I know it may seem far-fetched, but Jaycee saw a

big green car burning. Mike Smythe's green vintage Eldorado is missing. I saw it speeding away right before I found his body. No one has seen it since."

"Ivy, are you asking me to believe that this vision, or whatever it is, could lead to Mike Smythe's murderer?"

"I don't know John. All I can tell you is that Jaycee's visions are never wrong."

Garrett turned it over in his mind. What if it was true? He didn't have any solid leads. Well, this wasn't exactly a solid lead either, but it was something. His captain would go berserk if he found out that Garrett was even considering following this up. But he didn't have anything else; the Smythe family was breathing down the captain's neck, and the captain was breathing down his neck. He needed to think this over. He said goodbye to Ivy and Jaycee and went back to the station to contemplate his next move.

Whether John believed Jaycee or not it was hard to tell, but I knew Jaycee and she's always spot on. I couldn't just sit around waiting for him to decide if he would act or not. I had to see that murderer behind bars or my daughter might never be safe again. I picked up the phone and punched in the number for the local Army Recruiting Office. The phone was answered by Sergeant Dooley.

"Good afternoon, Sergeant," I began, "my name is Ivy Snow, and I'm calling to inquire about two young men who may have been recent recruits." I filled Dooley in, giving what details I had about Tommy and Ziggy. He checked his computer database and confirmed that both Tommy and Ziggy were recent recruits and they were now in boot camp at Fort Hood, Texas.

I thought about Jaycee's vision of the fire. There had been an awful lot of fires around here recently. Jim Kopeck's barn, the GM dealership, Joe's Bar and Grill, and now Morgan House. Jaycee said that Jim Kopeck was convinced that Tommy Monroe was responsible for the barn fire. Tommy was also our waiter at Joe's the day Jaycee and I almost died of smoke inhalation in the ladies room. There was nothing really to connect him to the dealership fire, except that he may have been working at Joe's the afternoon of Danny Gleason's meeting with Smythe. That brought us to Smythe. Again, no connection that I knew of, except maybe Joe's.

There could be a lot more that I didn't know about. I had to convince Garrett to investigate. I put on my favorite red windbreaker, hopped into the Z, and headed for the police station. When I arrived, I found John in his office, staring at the wall. Or maybe he wasn't staring at the wall, maybe he was staring at the framed photograph of former president Ronald Reagan that was hanging on it. He looked beat. I stepped through the door and spoke his name. He was visibly startled to see me standing there. "Ivy, what are you doing here?" he asked.

"John, I have to talk to you." I sat down on a hard oak chair in front of his desk. "I've been going over this whole thing, and I do believe that there is a connection between the rash of recent fires in the area, and the fire at Morgan House where Mike Smythe was murdered."

"How so?" he asked.

I told him about Jim Kopeck's suspicions regarding Tommy and Ziggy, my experience with the fire at Joe's, and about a possible connection to the fire at the GM dealership. "That, in combination with Jaycee's vision, leads me to wonder if somehow Ziggy Haskell and Tommy Monroe might be involved in all this. Ziggy's a little *slow*, if you know what I mean. He doesn't understand the consequences of his actions. We've seen that at the stable. At least there could be a possibility that he knows something that could help find the murderer."

"Okay, Ivy, maybe you have something there. Do you know where Haskell is now?"

"Yes, he's at Fort Hood, Texas, with his cousin Tommy. They're both recent Army recruits. Tommy sort of looks after Ziggy in a way, you know?"

Garrett called the captain and relayed his plan. The captain thought it was a bit far-fetched, but they had no other leads, and the pressure to solve this case was coming down pretty hard. He had no choice but to reluctantly approve Garrett's trip. Garrett got online and booked two tickets to Fort Hood for the next day. He would take a deputy with him just in case. He contacted the Army base and let them know of the arrangements that would be necessary. He went home and packed an overnight bag.

CHAPTER TWENTY-NINE

Bertrand Reynard stood in line for customs at JFK. He had booked a ticket for one to Côte d' Ivoire. He was traveling light; just his knapsack and satchel. He had crated the Hobart painting and shipped it separately. He could not afford to be caught with it in his possession. He turned things over in his mind. Perhaps he should not have left Wellington so soon. He really could have used Melinda's advice about selling the painting. After all, it would have to be done discreetly. He couldn't exactly put it in the window of an art gallery on Fifth Avenue, but with Mike Smythe dead he did not have the luxury of time.

He landed at Abidjan airport in Côte d' Ivoire at 2 in the morning. It had been a long and tiresome flight, and his anxiety didn't help. He had to sell that painting, and for a lot of money if he was going to get out of this mess. His compatriots were not known for their patience, and if he didn't come up with the money to finance this operation—well, he did not want to think about it. It didn't take long to get through customs since he only had two bags. He went to the cargo area and retrieved the Hobart. So far, so good. He had arranged for Renée to pick him up at ground transportation, so she should be along any moment now. Yes, here she was in her ancient blue Peugeot wagon. She pulled up to the curb; he opened the back hatch and loaded in his bags and the painting. He slid into the passenger seat and turned to her. She was more beautiful than he had remembered. Her hair was waist long, and so black that it shone with azure highlights. Her skin was a golden toffee, and she had those rare violet eyes, like Elizabeth Taylor.

"Renée, I have missed you," he said. She placed her hand on the back of his neck and drew him to her. They kissed with a passion that healed time and distance. The day that he married Renée was the happiest day of his life. A traffic guard motioned them to move on, so she slipped the car into the queue of slowly moving vehicles.

"Bertrand, is all well?" Renée asked. They had not been able to Skype for several days now and Renée was worried about him and the success of their plan.

"I am sorry to say that it is not at the moment, but we can make it so." He explained what happened over the past few days, and about the need to sell the painting.

"I know an art dealer in Cocody," she said. "He can sell the painting for us."

Bertrand breathed a sigh of relief. He should have known that he could count on Renée. They pulled up to the door of their apartment building, and were unexpectedly met by two of their associates from the terrorist organization. Bertrand's veins ran icy cold. How did they know where to find him? He invited them into the apartment; Renée stayed silent in the background.

"Bertrand, welcome back to Abidjan, my friend. How was your stay in America?"

"Americans are infidels!" Bertrand spat out his answer.

"Of course, of course. It must have been very easy for you to fool them. They are so gullible; like your little friend Melinda. She was only too pleased to help us locate you, the little fool."

Melinda! Bertrand swallowed hard. Melinda was responsible for leading these men to me. But how does she know where I am? Perhaps little Melinda is not as stupid as I thought.

The men sat down on the living room sofa and looked at Renée. She immediately went to the kitchen for beverages. "Now Bertrand, we are most anxious to learn how you have secured the money to fund our operation. Did you get it from Melinda, or from her friend Smythe?"

Bertrand took a deep breath. How would he ever explain... how would he get out of this alive? "The money will be coming as proceeds from the sale of Smythe's painting."

"What do you mean *will* be coming?"

Bertrand explained the difficulty he had in obtaining the cash, but he would get the cash when he sold Smythe's painting. The men did not look pleased.

"When will you have the money?"

"We are selling the painting in Cocody tomorrow. I will have the money by Friday," he said.

"See that you do." The men got up and walked out of the door just as Renée returned with the beverages.

The following day, they drove to Cocody to sell the painting. Bertrand stood as if frozen in the back of the gallery. He stared straight ahead, his eyes unseeing. Flashes of light bursting in his brain like fireworks in slow motion. Renée took a deep breath, trying to get her wits about her. "So, you are positive?" she asked the man.

"Oui, Madam, the painting is a forgery. A very good forgery, but a forgery all the same." Renée felt for Bertrand's hand and turned him to face her.

"Mon Dieu, Renée, mon Dieu," he said under his breath. The art dealer looked at the young couple and knew that what they were feeling was more than just disappointment. They turned around and slowly walked to the door as if in a trance. The dealer called after them, "Your painting... do not forget your painting!"

Bertrand and Renée stepped out onto the sidewalk, never looking back.

"What are we going to do?" he whispered.

"I do not know this minute," she said, "but we cannot go back to the apartment." They found the Peugeot parked along the curb where they had left it. They had to find a way out of this or they were as good as dead. They drove through the streets of Abidjan as if on autopilot. Suddenly, Renée had an idea. "We must go to America," she said. "You have friends there. Roberta, the landlady you stayed with, she can help us. We can hide with her until it's safe." As the words fell from her mouth, they both had the same thought. They would never be safe again. At least the terrorists would have a difficult time getting into the United States. They were on the FBI's most wanted list. Bertrand could think of no other solution. Fortunately, they both had their passports. Traveling without luggage would cause suspicion, but they could always say that their luggage had been stolen in the airport parking garage.

Bertrand took the next exit onto the highway and they headed for Abidjan International Airport. They abandoned the Peugeot on a side road not far from the airport. As they began to walk, Bertrand's thoughts turned to Smythe, and the painting. What a fool he had been. Knowing about Smythe as he did, he should have suspected that the painting was a fake, just like its owner.

They reached the airport, headed for the Air France ticket counter, and purchased two tickets to Paris with connections to JFK. The next plane would not be leaving for six hours. They walked to the gate, but what they saw when they arrived were three sets of coal black eyes boring into them. Their predators were lying in wait. Bertrand knew it was a fait accompli. Just then, his survival instinct and his adrenaline kicked in. He placed his hand on the small of Renee's back and shoved hard, propelling her into the group of men. The momentum scattered them all onto the ground.

Bertrand spun around and bolted down the hallway, headed for Ground Transportation. He slammed through the swinging glass doors and flew up the stairs to the sky tram platform. The Muslim men scrambled to their feet and took off after Bertrand, leaving Renée sprawled on the floor in their wake. They reached the doors just in time to see Bertrand board the sky tram as it zipped off down the track. They knew it was no use pursuing him. They ran back to the gate to confiscate Renée, but by then it was too late. She had disappeared into the crowd.

CHAPTER THIRTY

The young soldier sat on the steel Army-issue chair in a cinder-block room at Fort Hood, Texas. He slumped over with the weight of the world on his shoulders. How did he ever get here? This was the furthest he had ever been from his small-town home in Pennsylvania. As he waited for the detectives to arrive, he followed the shadows cast by the bare lightbulb hanging over his head. He couldn't think straight. With everything that happened the past couple of days his brain was all muddled up. All those assholes in Wellington—it was their own fault. Rich people always got away with everything; poor people got the shitty end of the stick.

Just then, two large men were ushered through the door. They wore regular suits, not Army uniforms, so they must be the detectives from back home. They introduced themselves and showed him their badges. Garrett and Ellis, two names he didn't recognize. They pulled up chairs to a long wooden table, and Garrett sat down. Ellis paced around the room taking it all in. "Son, we're here to see if you can give us any information on the events that happened recently in Wellington, Pennsylvania. You are from Wellington, right?"

"Yeah, that's right."

"When were you last there?"

"Oh, a while back, before I joined the Army."

"Did you hear about any fires that started around Wellington?" Garrett asked.

"There are a lot of fires there. Something is always burning."

"Did you know a man by the name of Michael Smythe?

This was it. He felt his throat tightening up. Shouldn't he have a lawyer, or something? Maybe you didn't get a lawyer if you were in the Army. He stared at his boots. Questions started coming at him like hard rain pounding on a tin roof. Did he know Smythe? Did he know that Smythe was dead? Did he know that Morgan House burned to the ground, like Jim Kopeck's barn? Did he know anything about a fire at the GM dealership, and the owner's death? Did he know that two women almost died of smoke inhalation at Joe's Bar and Grill? Did he know the whereabouts of the green vintage Cadillac Eldorado? Did he kill Michael Tellington Smythe?

It was no use. Ellis approached him with handcuffs. "You have the right to remain silent..." They lead Ziggy Haskell out of the room.

I kept my cell phone with me every moment waiting to hear from John. The call finally came. "Ivy, I'm calling from the airport in Texas. We have Zachariah Haskell in custody."

"Oh my God! Ziggy Haskell... you arrested him?"

"Yes, he confessed to the Smythe murder." Strangely enough, I was actually shocked now that I heard those words. I was pretty sure that Ziggy had something to do with the fires, but a confession of murdering Smythe? Wow!

"We are on our way back home, but I thought you'd want to know. Jaycee is safe now."

"Thank God." I took a deep breath and slowly let the air out of my lungs. I felt my body relax for the first time in I don't know how long. "Why did he do it, John?"

"I don't have all the facts yet, Ivy. We'll have to sort it all out when we get back."

I ran out to the stable looking for Jaycee. I wanted to tell her about Ziggy right away. I found her in Pirate's stall, working on the knots in his impressive mane. I slid the stall door open and stepped inside. "Hi, Jaycee honey. Listen, I have something to tell you." I wanted to be careful about how I handled this. I knew Jaycee would be upset. "I just got a call from Detective Garrett. Ziggy Haskell has been arrested for the murder of Mike Smythe."

"I know," she said.

"You know?"

"I saw it."

"Oh." I realized that she'd had a psychic vision.

"Mom, there's something wrong here. I could feel the evil that permeated Morgan House, but it's different—not the evil of murder."

"What do you mean, Jaycee?"

"I don't know, Mom... I don't know." She turned back to Pirate and grabbed another lock of mane.

Ziggy had a meeting scheduled with the public defender and he dreaded it. He hated lawyers in general, and he didn't want to answer any more questions. Bail had been set at $500,000 since they considered him a flight risk. Shit, he couldn't come up with $500 if he had to. His ass would remain in jail. In Ziggy's mind, public defenders were losers anyhow. If they were any good they'd be out making money hand over fist in some big law firm. The guard came to escort him to the interview room. He may as well get it over with. He knew that there was little hope for him anyway; everyone knew he was a big liar. They'd find him guilty and he'd die in the electric chair. It was just destiny that it would end up like this.

Wait a minute. Maybe he could make some kind

of a deal. Maybe if he confessed to setting those fires he wouldn't get the chair. That barn fire really was an accident. He didn't have anything to do with the dealership fire—that jackass Gleason did it himself. Still, he did set the fire at Joe's. Tommy didn't even see him put the Drano on Jaycee's burger. Rigging the door and setting the fire was a cinch. That little bitch Jaycee deserved everything she got for trying to pin shit on Tommy. It was too bad about her mom, though. Well, nobody died and Joe's is still standing. And Morgan House, why hell, that bastard Smythe was already dead. What did it matter about his house? Ziggy was beginning to get excited about the idea that he might get off altogether. He didn't actually kill anybody.

The door swung open, and this beautiful blonde walked in. She was wearing a white suit that closely follow the lines of her body; sexy, but not trashy. Wow! Maybe this wouldn't be so bad, after all. She sat down at the table across from him. He watched the door, waiting for the lawyer to walk through, but no one else came in. They were alone. Ziggy was confused. Who was this woman, and where was his lawyer? The young woman picked up on Ziggy's puzzled demeanor and proceeded to introduce herself. "Hello, Zachariah," she said offering a handshake. "I'm Victoria Edwards and I will be defending you."

Ziggy gaped at her. "You… you are my lawyer?"

He was incredulous. Lawyers were supposed to be nerdy dicks in pinstripe suits. Was it possible that she was for real?

"Yes, Zachariah, I'm your lawyer" Victoria said. He had to take a minute to think this over. She certainly was better than he expected, but in a way she made it harder. It didn't matter if she was the best lawyer in the world; he could never come clean with anybody like her. He was going down!

CHAPTER THIRTY-ONE

I opened the door and stepped into the night air. I walked down through my yard to the hammock that was strung between two giant Maple trees. I wiggled around to get comfortable, and gazed up at the black velvet sky exploding with stars. The night sky in the country is so vivid compared to the city. Less man-made light to interfere with God's creation.

I felt depressed. I failed Andy, poor soul. How could I not see that he was at his breaking point? I wasted time on a wild goose chase after Smythe when I should have been getting help for Andy. I thought about it; Ziggy Haskell sitting in jail on trial for murdering Mike Smythe—but why? That was the big question. How were those two connected? They came from different worlds. Ziggy was young and feisty; Smythe was old and stodgy. They didn't have the same friends or live in the same neighborhood. What brought them together that awful night?

I pulled out my cell and hit the speed dial for Crystal's number." Hi Crys, it's me."

"Hi Ivy, how are you? What's up?"

"I've been racking my brain over this Smythe murder. Did you know that Ziggy Haskell was arrested?"

"Yes, I heard about that," she said.

"I can't figure out for the life of me why Ziggy Haskell would murder Mike Smythe." Crystal was quiet for a moment. I could tell that she was deep in thought.

"I might be able to shed some light on that," she said. "While I was dating Biff Biddle, he told me that something funny was going on with Ziggy and his cousin Tommy Monroe. He didn't tell me what it was about, but I could tell that really rattled him."

I thought back to my meeting with Biddle earlier in the spring. He did say something about those boys. I tried to recall exactly what he said, but it was fuzzy. Something about destroying the Ice Festival? "Thanks Crys," I said. "I'll give you a call tomorrow, sleep tight."

"You too, Ivy. Don't drive yourself crazy over all this."

The next morning I drove to the school, determined to find out what Biddle knew. "Ivy Snow to see Mr. Biddle," I said to the intercom. The loud rasping buzzer sounded and I pulled the door open. I went straight to the office and told the secretary that I would like to meet with Mr. Biddle. She said that he was teaching a gym class the moment, but the period would be ending soon. I went out into the hallway and sat down on a hard plastic chair to check my email while I waited.

A few minutes later Biff poked his head around the corner and asked me to come into his office. He was wearing a red and black sweat suit—the official school colors. We sat facing each other and I stared into his weak, watery blue eyes. "Mr. Biddle, I'm here to talk to you about some former students of yours, Ziggy Haskell and his cousin, Tommy Monroe." That statement was met with stony silence. Biddle didn't move a muscle. "You remember them, don't you?"

"Yeah, I remember," he said.

"The last time we met you mentioned them to me, you said something about their vandalizing the sculptures at the Ice Festival, but there's more to it than that, isn't there, Mr. Biddle?"

"What do you mean?" Biddle squirmed in his seat.

"Did you know that Ziggy Haskell was arrested for the murder of William Tellington Smythe?"

"I heard," Biff mumbled.

I decided to go straight for the jugular. "Well, what are you going to do about it? You know a lot more about that kid and what was going on in his life. After all, you were his guidance counselor."

"Ms. Snow, what my students tell me is confidential."

"Not in this case, Mr. Biddle. Not when it's a matter of murder. After all, you are not a lawyer, or priest."

Biff sprang up from his chair and thrust his body forward to get in my face. The *Little Napoleon* complex at its best. "Listen lady, who do you think you are coming in here and telling me how to do my job?" he railed.

Good, I thought, I had him on the defensive. "Obviously somebody has to. I am a mother and I protect children."

"I can't be responsible for every snot-nose kid that gets into trouble." He was practically shouting at me.

"Trouble? What kind of trouble did Ziggy get into?"

"He's a little liar. You can't believe anything that son-of-a-bitch says." Biff was breathing heavily and his face was scarlet.

"What did he tell you, Mr. Biddle? What did he tell you?" I pressed on relentlessly.

"He said that Smythe was a rapist." Biff's eyes grew wide realizing that he had let the dirty secret slip out.

They were at his house all the time, and he'd invite them in saying that he would give them a bottle of beer. Most of them rode his bus occasionally, so they thought he was okay. I guess the kids went in and drank the beer, got drunk, and that's when Smythe did it."

I felt nauseous. How could any decent man do that to a child? How evil and depraved does one have to be to harm an innocent young boy that way? "What did you do about it, Mr. Biddle?"

"I told him to just forget about it."

"What?" I couldn't believe my ears.

"Listen, Smythe was a rich and powerful man, well-connected. The kid was from the wrong side of the tracks. Who'd believe a story like that?" I could hear the guilty pleading in Biff's voice. I gathered up my things and bolted out of the office, slamming the door behind me. I was shaking with anger. I had to get out of there before I throttled that bastard. God, I couldn't believe that Crystal was ever in love with that coward. What should I do now that I had discovered the motive? What would a jury do with that? Could the D.A. get him off? I needed to think. I got in my Z and flew back to Little Paddocks. Deep down, I knew what I had to do.

As soon as I got to the house, I ran to the bathroom and splashed ice cold water on my face. I had to get a grip on myself. Ziggy's lawyer had to be told what I just learned, it was his only chance. I heard a car coming up the gravel drive and I peered out the window to see Jaycee's riding instructor dropping her off after her lesson. She came bounding through the door, but stopped short when she saw my face. "Mom, what's the matter?" I must have been white as a ghost. Whether or not to tell Jaycee the truth about what I now knew was a dilemma. It was so horrific; she was so young. Just hearing about something like that happening to someone you know, right in your own town, was enough to infect any child's psyche.

But Jaycee wasn't just any child. Because of her "gift" she has been exposed to an ugliness of human nature that no child her age should have to experience. "Jaycee, I have learned something truly heinous."

"What is it, Mom?"

I took a deep breath. "I know the reason why Mike Smythe was murdered."

"Why?" She murmured.

"Because when Ziggy and his cousin Tommy were young boys Mike Smythe raped them, and who knows how many others."

Jaycee was stunned. Her hands flew up to cover her face. "Oh my God, Mom... oh my God!"

I rushed over to her and held her in my arms. "I have to get to the D.A. and tell her what I know. It may be Ziggy's only chance to avoid the death penalty."

"I want to go with you!"

I thought about that momentarily. It probably wasn't a good idea, but I couldn't leave her here alone to try and cope with this nightmare. "Okay, honey, let's go to the courthouse."

We climbed into the Yukon, drove to the courthouse and lucked out finding an available parking meter on the street right out in front.

Jaycee and I were shown into Victoria Edwards's office at the Ashland County courthouse. I swear that the same architect must design every county courthouse in the east. A large rotunda, marble floors throughout, and thick oak paneling covering every wall. Ashland was no different.

"Good afternoon Ms. Edwards. My name is Ivy Snow, and this is my daughter, Jaycee."

"Please sit down, ladies, and do call me Victoria. I was told that you have information on the Haskell case that you would like to share with me."

"Yes, I do." I proceeded to tell her the story given to me by Biff Biddle. She slowly shook her head back and forth. Attorneys in her position hear a lot of terrible things. I know that it didn't make it any easier on her.

"Well, there's the answer." She sighed. "I knew his motive had to be compelling. Try as I might, I couldn't get anything out of Zachariah. Biff Biddle's right about one thing, it's a hard story to swallow. One of Wellington's most upright citizens—to have done something like that. Ms. Snow, even though it's true, coming from you it's just hearsay."

"Yes, Victoria, but you could get Biff Biddle to testify," I said.

"Biddle's testimony would be hearsay as well, since he didn't witness the act."

We looked each other in the eye, and I realized that what she was trying to tell me was that we would have to get the story straight from Ziggy himself. That might be difficult. Because of the nature of the motive he might not be willing to come forward. Rape victims are often unjustly filled with guilt and shame and often with denial, which I was sure was true in Ziggy's case.

"We will need to talk to Zachariah," Victoria said. She picked up the phone and buzzed the jail, asking that he be brought to the interview room. She took me aside. "Do you think it's a good idea for your daughter to come with us, Ms. Snow?"

I knew what she was thinking, of course. I explained about Jaycee's psychic gifts and she agreed that in this case it would be all right. We walked into the jail, which was conveniently located right next to the courthouse. When we got to the interview room Ziggy was already there, dressed in an orange jumpsuit.

"Good afternoon, Zachariah," the lawyer said. She introduced Jaycee and me, but of course we were already acquainted with Ziggy from the Wellington Riding Academy. She skillfully unveiled the facts that we had learned about his past with Mike Smythe. Ziggy turned his head to the side and refused to look at us, although we could see his skin turning beet red.

All of a sudden, Jaycee stood up. She had that trance-like look on her face that accompanies her psychic visions. She mouthed the name DALE. Ziggy's head whipped around, his eyes shooting daggers at Jaycee.

"What's going on?" Victoria asked.

Jaycee blinked her eyes, and slowly began pacing

up and down the length of the room." I see Dale Monroe," she says quietly. "He is riding on a school bus. Mr. Smythe is driving the school bus."

Ziggy shot up from his chair. "Stop! Shut your mouth right now!" Jaycee shook her head and was back in the room with the rest of us.

"Zachariah, what is it?" Victoria asked.

Ziggy's face was pure rage. "I'll kill that Smythe. I'll kill that son of a bitch."

"Zachariah, Smythe is already dead," she said.

"If he touches one hair on my cousin Dale's head, I'll see him burn in hell!"

CHAPTER THIRTY-TWO

The headlines in the Wellington Gazette read: *District Attorney Files Murder In the First Degree Against Zachariah Haskell.* The case was getting a lot of press since the murder victim was a prominent citizen in the community. Anyone who knew Ziggy would consider the possibility that he was guilty, but it really didn't matter. What mattered was that Smythe was dead and somebody had to pay. The Field & Stream Club smelled blood, and formed a conspiracy to keep quiet about the photo of Smythe that they had received anonymously. After all, he was the victim—why sully his reputation on top of everything else? It was that lowlife Haskell and his kind that caused all the trouble in this world. Upright citizens, such as themselves, were in constant danger from their brutality.

Months passed, and finally the trial was set for December first, happy holidays. I dreaded the whole thing, but in a way I was anxious for it to start—and end. The presiding judge in the case was Leonard P. Clancy, "Lenny the Letch" as he was known around the club. He was old, short and skeletal, and he had teeth so yellow that they looked like corn kernels in his mouth. You prayed that he wouldn't have a reason to smile.

I got to the courthouse early. This was not my first murder trial; I had sat in on many of Bart's cases. I wanted to make sure that I got a decent seat, anticipating that this trial would be a circus. I wasn't wrong. The first part of the trial would be about jury selection, which on the surface might seem tedious, but when it came right down to it the outcome of the entire case rested with the twelve people who would be chosen right here and now. It would have been impossible to see anyone from Wellington on that jury since everybody there would have a connection to the victim, or the accused, in one way or another. All twelve jurors, six men and six women, were from the other side of the county.

I glanced around the courtroom and saw a lot of familiar faces. Melinda was there, of course, as well as Biff Biddle and Jim Kopeck. Suddenly, there was a loud bang and the court was in session. Judge Lenny entered the room and climbed into his enormous chair behind the bench. Ziggy entered through the door on the left side of the room accompanied by two imposing bailiffs. He was dressed in a badly cut brown polyester suit, but it wouldn't have mattered if it was Hugo Boss. Ziggy was just one of those guys that look totally uncomfortable and out of place in a suit and tie. His face was haggard and his demeanor was hopeless. He took his seat at the defense table next to Victoria Edwards. Victoria, in contrast to Ziggy, was dressed in a meticulously tailored black pantsuit with a leopard print blouse. She looked the essence of confidence and competence. She leaned over and whispered something to Ziggy. He wiggled, then sat up straight in his chair.

The prosecuting attorney assigned to the case, Paul Ponzi, was a middle-aged man. He was balding and tried to disguise the fact with a bad comb-over, as so many men do. The shoulders of his navy blue jacket were sprinkled with dandruff, and he wore a permanently stained green necktie. He didn't look like a very formidable adversary, but he had been with the D.A.'s office for over twenty-five years and he knew his way around a courtroom.

Judge Lenny asked counsel to approach the bench and laid down the ground rules for his courtroom. No unnecessary arguing, no theatrics, and please, a fervent reverence for starting the lunch hour on time. Lenny had his priorities. For many unfamiliar with the judicial system it is believed that justice has something to do with the law. This assumption is blatantly wrong. The proceedings of the day in a courtroom are at the whim of the individual judge, and on the side of the bed from which he or she arose that morning.

The prosecution was offered first opening remarks. Ponzi stood, rubbed his hands together slowly, and approached the jury box. "Ladies and gentlemen of the jury, we are here today to prove that Zachariah

Haskell"—he turned around and glared at Ziggy—"is responsible for the brutal murder of Michael Tellington Smythe, one of Wellington, Pennsylvania's leading citizens. We will prove beyond the shadow of a doubt that Zachariah Haskell, with malice aforethought, bludgeoned to death Mr. Smythe, then set his house on fire and escaped by stealing the victim's automobile." Ponzi paused for breath and effect. "The state will show you, ladies and gentlemen of the jury, a young man so depraved, his soul so saturated with the black sinfulness of hate and jealousy, that he was compelled to destroy Michael Tellington Smythe, whose very life exemplified the success, social position, and respect that Mr. Haskell could never hope to achieve." The jury stared wide-eyed at Ponzi. Silence permeated the room. Ponzi turned and sauntered back to his seat, looking quite smug.

It was now Victoria's turn. She'd been a public defender for three years, joining the department soon after passing the bar. She was a quick study and knew Ponzi's reputation for winning cases by coming through the back door. She knew to keep a very close eye on him and to never underestimate him. She began her opening remarks by crafting a very sympathetic narrative of the life of Zachariah Haskell. Born to a single mother out-of-wedlock, he grew up in a section of Wellington populated by rusting trailers, salvage yards, and long-abandoned warehouses.

Zachariah was not a child of fancy private schools, polo lessons, and country clubs. He was a child of poverty, hardship, and condescending looks. Victoria paused. But those were not the building blocks of Zachariah's character. Zachariah was a young man who seized the opportunities offered him by the fine education provided by the Wellington school system. He took advantage of the opportunities afforded him for employment at the Wellington Equestrian Center, and ultimately sought to better himself and serve his country in the United States armed forces.

It was because he was from the wrong side of the tracks that the murder was pinned on him. He was an easy mark. Victoria would prove that it was not Zachariah Haskell, but another who took the life of Michael Tellington Smythe.

CHAPTER THIRTY-THREE

Tommy Monroe sat on his bunk in the barracks at Fort Hood reading the latest edition of *Stars and Stripes*, the official news publication of the U.S. Army. There was an article on page three about Ziggy's arrest for murder and about his trial, which was underway in Ashland County. Tommy finished the article and flung the paper across the room. He buried his head in his hands and fought back tears. What was he doing here? What was he doing at Fort Hood when his cousin Ziggy was fighting for his life? Tommy reached under his bed and pulled out his knapsack. He began stuffing socks, underwear, shirts and pants in at a frantic pace. He had made up his mind. He was going to Pennsylvania.—leave or no leave. He had to!

Tommy managed to get off the base without creating suspicion. He had no mode of transportation other than hitchhiking, so he headed for the nearest highway going east and stuck out his thumb. For once, Tommy got lucky. A large eighteen-wheeler pulled over to the side of the road and stopped next to him. The driver stuck his head out of the passenger-side window and asked Tommy where he was headed. The driver told him to hop in; he was on his way to Harrisburg, Pennsylvania, and would be going right through

Wellington. Tommy climbed up into the cab and was surprised to find it was quite luxurious. The driver, whose name was Mickey, was the owner-operator and virtually spent his life in that cab. He had to have some of the creature comforts.

The two men struck up an easy conversation, Tommy careful not to reveal his reason for going to Wellington. They talked football, mostly Steelers and Cowboys; some politics—the country was going to hell in a handbasket—and Mickey's soon-to-be final divorce from his second wife, Wanda Lea. It made the time go faster, but they were still hundreds of miles from Pennsylvania, and time was of the essence with Ziggy's life hanging by a thread.

As they crossed the border into North Carolina, the radio crackled with a special weather emergency announcement. "We interrupt this program to alert listeners in the Charlotte area of an approaching windstorm with gusts up to eighty miles per hour. We recommend that you seek shelter in a secure place and avoid going out if at all possible." Tommy looked over at Mickey, waiting for his reaction. Mickey was quiet and seemed unconcerned. "Hey man, is that gonna cause problems?" Tommy asked.

Mickey shrugged. "Really can't tell—should be over by the time we reach Charlotte." Tommy sighed, thinking *damn well hope so.*

They drove on through the night heading north. Tommy awoke to loud banging sounds and raging gusts of wind. Startled, he looked over at Mickey who was gripping the steering wheel, keeping a laser focus on the windshield in front of him.

"What's going on, man?" Tommy could hear the fear in his own voice.

"We're stuck in a traffic jam right in the middle of that windstorm. This is crazy." Mickey's breathing was shallow.

As Tommy gazed out the window he saw a sight like nothing he had seen before. Traffic was bumper-to-bumper on the ridge, but mostly tractor-trailers, some of which were literally swaying in the wind. The force of the wind was so great that any trailer without a full load was fighting to stay upright. Not everyone made it. Tommy watched as the mighty tractor-trailers were thrown over sideways left and right. They tumbled off the road and down the steep grade into a ravine that was bottomless in the pitch dark of night. Tommy grabbed hold of the armrest on his seat. He couldn't believe the scene before him. He looked over at Mickey, who was ghostly pale and had a death grip on the wheel. He had panic in his eyes.

"Mickey, what should we do?" Tommy screamed.

Mickey shot Tommy a quick glance. "Pray...we're carrying a light load."

Just then the huge truck began to sway from side

to side. Tommy had the sensation of being on a wild ride at Six Flags. He felt the truck tip over—and that was all.

Tommy tried to open his eyes but the lids were so heavy they felt as though they were sewn shut. He tried again, and saw a sliver of light above him. It hurt. He heard the sound of voices somewhere nearby, but he couldn't hear what they were saying. Just then he felt someone take his hand. Who was it? Where was he? As the fogginess in his brain began to clear, he tried to make out the words buzzing around him.

"He's waking up. He's coming out of the coma… thank God!"

What? Was he in a coma? What happened? He didn't remember anything. He tried to think, but he couldn't. He closed his heavy eyelids again and fell into a deep dark sleep.

CHAPTER THIRTY-FOUR

Day two of Ziggy's trial was accosted by a blustery Allegheny mountain snowstorm. I trudged through eight inches of the stuff that had drifted onto my driveway to reach the Yukon. It's always smart to have a brush and ice scraper for these occasions, but the fact that I left them inside the vehicle was problematic. I had to yank repeatedly on the frozen truck door to get it open. Unfortunately, that caused the snow on the door and window to fly inside, coating the driver seat—great. I turned on the engine to get it warmed up and started sweeping and scraping the exterior. Ten minutes later, I was ready to get behind the wheel and head for the courthouse. I only hoped that everyone else was late as well. I didn't want to miss anything important.

As I entered the courtroom, Ponzi called his first witness, Detective John Garrett of the Pennsylvania State Police. Garrett was looking good today. He was wearing a dark blue pinstriped suit, a white shirt with French cuffs, and a soft blue foulard tie. Quite elegant for a police detective. I noticed that he had gotten a haircut since the last time I saw him, and his demeanor and mannerisms seemed different. More polished, more distinguished. This must be the "courtroom" Garrett, as opposed to the "street" Garrett. After he was sworn in, and his credentials duly recorded by the court stenographer, Ponzi approached the witness stand and paced slowly back and forth.

"Detective Garrett, you were the arresting officer in this case, were you not?"

"Yes," Garrett replied with clarity.

"Could you please tell the court the circumstances which led you to arrest Zachariah Haskell?"

Garrett gazed around the courtroom, seeking eye contact with Ziggy. "The Wellington police were investigating a rash of fires in the area that started last spring. Their main suspect was Zachariah Haskell. The fire that destroyed Morgan House the night Smythe was murdered had the same M.O., and that led me to suspect Haskell. I found out that he was AWOL from Fort Hood that night so I started tracking him down."

Garrett was reluctant to talk about Jaycee's vision of the soldiers and the burning car. Although it did play a part in leading him to Haskell, he still wasn't sure how much he believed in the whole psychic thing. It was probably a coincidence. The kid probably had a dream or something. Maybe she just had strong intuition.

"Then what did you do?" Ponzi asked.

"I contacted Fort Hood and found out that Haskell had returned, so I flew down there to question him."

"And what was the result of that interview?"

"Haskell confessed to setting the Wellington fires. He said that he was angry because those dumb rich bastards, as he called them, got everything. Money, cars, houses. He got nothing."

"Did he confess to the Smythe murder?"

"He did at first, but then he changed his story. He admitted to torching Morgan House, but he says he didn't kill Smythe."

"Did he say if he knew who did kill Smythe?"

"No, he said that he thought Smythe died in the fire. When he found out the Smythe was killed by trauma to the head with a blunt instrument, he figured that Smythe was dead before he set the house on fire."

"So Haskell now denies that he killed Smythe?"

"Yes, he says he's not guilty."

"And what is your professional opinion, Detective?"

"I think he's guilty. I think Smythe came home and surprised Haskell while he was setting the fire. There was a struggle, and Haskell bashed him over the head with the pendulum from the grandfather clock. There was no sign of anyone else there that night."

"Thank you, Detective, that will be all the questions for now. Your witness, Ms. Edwards."

Victoria approached the witness stand holding the long brass object tagged as evidence. "Detective Garrett, do you recognize this?" she asked.

"Yes. It's a pendulum from an old grandfather's clock. It looks like the object that killed Smythe."

"When was the first time you saw this?" Victoria asked.

"That night, at the scene of the murder. The Wellington police took it out of the house when they brought out Smythe's body. The blood on it was fresh then, a dark red."

"So that's how you concluded that it was the murder weapon?"

"That, and the fact that the DNA test proves it was Smythe's blood."

Victoria looked at the jury, trying to decipher their expressions. They were hanging on Garrett's every word—and they believed him.

"Detective Garrett, did you find anything else on the pendulum? Fingerprints? Skin or hair samples?"

"No, we didn't, just the blood."

"Smythe's blood?"

"Yes."

"Is there any physical evidence that Zachariah Haskell killed Michael Smythe?"

"No."

"Thank you, Detective, that will be all."

I thought that Victoria scored points with the jury regarding the murder weapon, but Garrett was pretty convincing, too. Ponzi rose from his chair and called

Officer Blaine Stewart of the Wellington police to the stand. Stewart was the first officer to arrive at the murder scene. He was a rookie on the force, and had been hired six months ago right out of the Police Academy. He's young and good-looking, earning him the nickname "Officer Handsome" among the women of Wellington. Stewart was the first officer to arrive at the scene of the crime. He had been cruising around the neighborhood on his usual rounds, when he passed by Morgan House and saw flames shooting up from the back of the house. He immediately patched into the Wellington Fire Department and then called for backup.

"Officer Stuart, what did you find when you went into Morgan House on the night of the murder?"

"I walked through the front door, which was wide open, and I saw a woman struggling to drag someone out of the house."

"What did you do then?"

"I went in and put my hand on her shoulder. I sort of pushed her out through the front door, then I grabbed Smythe under the arms and dragged his body outside. I laid him on the grass and checked for vital signs. He was dead."

"And where was the woman?"

"She was standing right behind us looking shocked and confused."

"Did you see anyone else?"

"No."

"Then what happened?"

"By then, the fire department arrived, and so did my backup."

"Okay, Officer Stuart. One more thing. When you went into the room where you found the body, did you notice anything unusual?" Ponzi was fishing, hoping that Stewart would mention something to incriminate Haskell.

"Yes, I did. A big grandfather clock was all smashed up. Part of it, the pendulum, was lying on the floor next to Mr. Smythe's body. I went inside and grabbed it and took it out with me."

Tell us something we don't already know, thought Ponzi. This guy was a waste of time. "Thank you, Officer Stuart, that will be all." Ponzi turned and looked at Victoria. "Your witness, counselor."

"No questions," she said.

CHAPTER THIRTY-FIVE

I decided to stop at the post office on my way home from court to retrieve the mail that had been piling up over the past few days. Oh, good! The latest issue of *Architectural Digest* had arrived, along with the new *Seventeen* for Jaycee. I shuffled through a bunch of junk mail, and an official-looking envelope jumped out at me. I tore it open to find a summons. I was being subpoenaed to testify for the prosecution in the Michael Tellington Smythe case. I wasn't surprised. After all, I found the body, so of course I would have to testify. God—how do I get myself into these things?

I negotiated the icy roads back to Little Paddocks in my trusty Yukon. Heaven knows the Z could never have handled this. I walked through the front door to find an unusually quiet house. Jayson would be at swim practice, so I didn't expect to see him. But where was Jaycee? I was usually met with blasting rock music or a blaring TV show. "Jaycee... Jaycee where are you?" No answer. I walked through the house and went to check her room. I found her lying on her bed, staring at the ceiling. "Jaycee, honey, how are you?" She didn't answer. "Is everything all right?"

"Mom, I just had a really weird dream."

"What was it, honey?"

"I dreamed that I was on a mountaintop with hundreds of giant trucks. Suddenly, the trucks began sprouting wings and they were flying high up into the sky. Human bodies began falling out of the trucks, splattering all over the ground. It freaked me out, Mom."

I sat and listened to her intently as she went on. "Then, a body fell next to me. I tried to run, but it reached out and grabbed me. It was Tommy Monroe and he was covered in bandages like a mummy. He said, 'Hello, Charlotte.' I said, 'My name's not Charlotte.' Just then I looked down to see you and Detective Garrett running up the mountain toward us. I woke up."

Jaycee has had some strange dreams before, but this one was a whopper. "Do you know what the dream means, Jaycee?"

"I'm not sure, but I feel like Tommy Monroe is trying to tell me something. He's hurt—he's been in an accident and was almost killed. He's far away from home, but he's trying to reach home."

I didn't know how any of this mattered at the moment, but I knew that somehow it did. I picked up the phone and dialed Garrett's number.

"Hello, John, I need to talk to you about something that might be important to the Smythe case. I don't want to discuss it over the phone."

"Okay, meet me at the Perk Me Up Café in half an

hour," Garrett said, hungry for any news that could shed light on this case.

I hung up the phone and went to my room for a quick touch-up. I wished I had time for a shower; something about being in court always makes me feel grimy. On the way to the Perk Me Up, I turned on my car radio to the news station. All the usual stories: robberies, bribery, arrests. Then came a story that caught my attention. It was a report from Charlotte, North Carolina. Charlotte—the second time I'd heard that name within the hour. What most people would pass off as a coincidence, I honed in on. It's something you learn to do instinctively when you live with a psychic. Charlotte? What was going on in Charlotte?

The announcer reported on a violent windstorm that swept through the mountainous regions of North Carolina, near Charlotte, and claimed the lives of five tractor-trailer drivers and seriously injured several more. The hundred-mile per hour winds caught empty trailers and those carrying light loads, and literally swept them off the highway, sending them tumbling down into the ravine below.

Oh, my God, what a horrible sight it must have been. Huge tractor-trailers flying through the air. Wow, flying trucks, injured bodies... Charlotte. Wait a minute, the pieces were coming together. I met Garrett at the

Perk Me Up and relayed my story. Reluctantly, he pulled out his cell phone and dialed his contact at Fort Hood.

CHAPTER THIRTY-SIX

Ponzi rose from his chair at the prosecutors table and called Dr. Herman Deal to the stand. Dr. Deal is the Ashland County coroner and has been for the past 40 years. His scalp is in an advanced state of baldness, and his eyes require glasses with lenses so thick they remind me of old-fashioned Coke bottles. He's almost a caricature of a forensic pathologist, but make no mistake about it, he's a man who knows his stuff.

"Dr. Deal, did you have an opportunity to examine the body of William Tellington Smythe at the scene of the death?"

"Yes, I did, the police called me as soon as the body was discovered."

"What was your assessment then?"

"Rigor mortis had not yet set in, so that told me that Smythe had been dead for less than an hour."

Ponzi ambled back and forth in front of the witness stand. "And what did you determine was the cause of death?"

"Mr. Smythe was bludgeoned to death about the head and neck with a blunt instrument."

"Was death instantaneous?"

"No. Mr. Smythe died of a cerebral hemorrhage,

which would have taken fifteen to twenty minutes. "

"So Doctor, there was nothing to indicate that he died of smoke inhalation?"

"There was smoke damage found in his lungs, so it may have contributed to the death, but the brain hemorrhage was the ultimate cause."

"Was there anything else about Smythe's body that would provide this court with insight into Mr. Smythe's death?"

"Alcohol was found in his bloodstream, which would have meant that he'd been drinking within several hours of his death."

Melinda's head shot up and her eyes grew wide as saucers.

"Is there anything else, Doctor?"

"Yes. A sperm ejaculation was found on his upper thigh and groin area, which indicated that Mr. Smythe had sex, or attempted to have sex, within an hour of his death."

Melinda gasped. Spectators turned to look at her. She turned red and quickly lowered her head and pretended to be digging for something in her purse. Oh, my God! The alcohol in Mike's bloodstream could be explained by the drinks that they had earlier that evening. But semen! Who would he be having sex with? Melinda thought of Bertrand and her veins ran icy cold. He must have been there when she dropped Mike off.

That S.O.B.! Did he have sex with Mike, kill him, and then steal the painting? But what about the fire? Ziggy admitted to setting that. Were they both at Morgan House at the same time? Did they see each other? Did they plan this together? Melinda's mind whirled.

Ponzi turned the witness over to Victoria. She was livid. That piece of information about the semen had not been submitted to her during discovery. Dirty pool. Well, if that's the way they wanted to play.

"Dr. Deal, you testified that Mr. Smythe died from blunt force trauma to his head and neck. Was there any indication as to whether the blows were administered from the front or from the back of Smythe's body?"

"No. He could have been attacked from any angle and been beaten continually on the back side of his body after he fell to the floor."

"I see. Doctor, is there any way of telling whether or not Smythe's assailant was a man or woman?"

"No."

"Is there any way to determine if the killer was right-handed or left-handed?"

"No, it could be either."

"Thank you, Doctor, that will be all for now." Victoria walked back to the defendant's table and sat next to Ziggy. He was pale as a ghost. The reality of the situation was sinking in. They would find him guilty and he was going to the electric chair. Where the hell was

Tommy?

I paced up and down the hall outside of the courtroom waiting for the trial to reconvene. I knew that I would be the next witness and I dreaded it to the point of nausea. My cell phone rang and I looked down to see it was Garrett calling. "Hello John, what's going on?"

"Hello Ivy. I got a hold of the guys down at Fort Hood, and guess what? Monroe is missing. He disappeared from the base three days ago."

Just then, the bailiff came to inform me the court was reconvening, and that I was the next witness up.

"John, I can't talk now, I'm being called back into court to testify. I'll call you back as soon as possible. Oh, you might want to start your search for Monroe around Charlotte, North Carolina."

I ran my fingers through my hair, stood up as tall as possible, and followed the bailiff into the courtroom.

CHAPTER THIRTY-SEVEN

As the trial progressed, the number of spectators coming to see the show doubled. All the usual suspects were there, including Melinda, Biff Biddle and, what do you know, Crystal was here today. She was probably hoping to see Biff sweat it out on the witness stand. To my surprise, there was a new face in the crowd, Sloane Parker. I was glad to see her, and waved across the room. She waved back and gave me the thumbs up. It felt good having her there for support, but I also wondered if she had any news of Bart.

I could feel all eyes on me as I took the witness stand and was sworn in. Having been married to a criminal defense lawyer, I knew that there are many attributes that contribute to the perceived credibility of the witness. Appearance is a major one, so I had selected a dark navy suit with a cream silk blouse and understated gold jewelry. I wanted to convey honesty and confidence; after all, Ziggy's life hung in the balance. I watched Ponzi move slowly toward me, not liking him one little bit. He was a snake in the grass in the courtroom, and probably one out of the courtroom, too.

"Ms. Snow, you are the person who found Michael Tellington Smythe's body. Is that not true?"

I answered a simple "yes." The first rule of testifying is to make sure that you fully understand the question. The second rule is to never elaborate. Ponzi stared into my eyes and I felt my skin crawl.

"Could you please tell the jury how you happened to come upon the victim?"

"I was walking by his house and I noticed that the door was standing wide open, so I went inside and found Smythe lying on the floor."

"Then what did you do?"

"I went over to check and see if he was dead or alive."

"And what did you determine, Ms. Snow?"

"I was trying to find a pulse when I looked up and saw that the kitchen was on fire, so I started trying to drag Smythe out of the house."

"And did you?"

"No, he was too heavy; but just then the police arrived and pulled him out."

"Did you see anyone else in the house when you arrived?"

"No."

"Ms. Snow, how did you happen to be passing by Morgan House on the night of the murder?"

"I was on my way to the Coach House B&B, looking for the intern who was working at my company."

"And who would that be?" For Ponzi, it must have

felt like he was pulling teeth.

"His name is Bertrand Reynard." I saw Melinda squirm in her seat.

"When Smythe's body was pulled from the fire, who was at the scene?"

"Beside the police and firemen, Roberta Bristol, the owner of the Coach House, was there."

"Did Mr. Reynard show up at the scene?"

"No, he did not."

"Ms. Snow, are you aware that on the night of the murder Mr. Smythe's green Cadillac Eldorado went missing?"

My thoughts flashed back to the scene of Mike's car speeding away from Morgan House as I arrived. "I saw the car being driven away from the house. At first I thought it was Mike Smythe driving."

"But it wasn't, was it, Ms. Snow? As we know now, Mike Smythe was lying dead inside the house. Do you have any idea who might have been driving that car?"

"No."

"That will be all for now, Ms. Snow. Your witness, Ms. Edwards."

Victoria stood up. "Ms. Snow, do you know the whereabouts of Bertrand Reynard at this time?"

"No I don't."

"That will be all for now." Victoria sat down and scribbled a note on her legal pad.

I stepped down from the witness stand and went back to my seat in the gallery. Ponzi picked up a stack of papers from his table. "Your Honor, I would like to call Roberta Bristol."

Roberta walked quickly to the stand. This was the kind of drama she lived for. She loved being the center of attention and this was about as good as it got. She scanned the jury box to make sure that they were fully intrigued by her presence.

"Mrs. Bristol, would you please state your full name, address, and occupation for the court?"

Roberta happily told them who she was, her address, and her position as owner and proprietress of the Coach House B&B on East Main Street in Wellington, Pennsylvania.

"Mrs. Bristol, your establishment is located right next door to Morgan House, is it not?"

"Well, it was—before Morgan House burned down, that is. That heap of cinders next door is an eyesore that is devaluing my property. Mike Smythe was always complaining that the color of my B&B was ruining the ambiance of the street. Well, now they'll be no argument that the remnants of Morgan House is making East Main look just hideous." Apparently, Roberta never learned the second rule for giving testimony.

Ponzi rolled his eyes." Ms. Bristol, were you and Michael Smythe friendly?"

Roberta considered this question. What did he mean by "friendly?" Everyone knew of the bad blood between them, especially after Smythe filed that complaint about the color of her B&B. Roberta worried that if she told him what she really thought of Smythe that they would consider her a suspect in the murder. "We were neighbors, but we kept ourselves to ourselves." She thought that sounded noncommittal enough.

"Mrs. Bristol, when was the last time you saw Smythe alive?"

"It was earlier that evening. I saw him and his lady friend"—she spoke Melinda's name—"leaving the house and driving away in her car."

"Mrs. Bristol, do you have any idea where they were going?"

"No, of course not. I didn't keep tabs on Michael Smythe. They could have been going anywhere."

"Did you see them return?"

"No, but now that I think back on it, I did see Bertrand Reynard, he's a guest at the Coach, you know. He went into Mike Smythe's house. He walked right in, so I just assumed that Smythe was at home."

"Did you see Mr. Reynard leave?"

"No, I didn't."

A lightbulb went off in my head. Pieces of the puzzle were coming together. There were things that Victoria needed to know—and fast.

"Mrs. Bristol, were you aware of any other visitors at Morgan House?"

"Well, I'm not a busybody you know, but I did find it strange that so many fellows stopped in to visit him. I didn't know any of them, but then again we didn't travel in the same social circles."

"What about domestic help? Did he have a cook, or a maid?"

"Well, I know that Betsy Quinn came in to clean for him once a week." Roberta thought about seeing Ziggy Haskell doing odd jobs around the place. She didn't know whether or not she should mention that because Ziggy was on trial and she didn't think he was guilty. Those kids are no-goodniks , but murder? She didn't think so.

"Mrs. Bristol, did you see anyone else?"

Roberta panicked. She had better tell the truth—they were bound to find out anyway and, after all, it wasn't her job to protect Ziggy Haskell. If he didn't do it, he would be found innocent and that was that. "Well, Mr. Ponzi, I did see Ziggy—I mean, Zachariah Haskell over there, doing some yardwork and odd jobs. But that was awhile back, way before he joined the Army."

"Did you see Haskell over there often?"

"Not really." Roberta had told the truth, but she needn't add fuel to the fire.

"Thank you, that's all for now, Mrs. Bristol."

Roberta breathed a sigh of relief. The D.A. hadn't

asked any questions about cross-dressing. That detective might not have told him—but even if he had, Ponzi probably wouldn't want to bring it up.

After all, he was trying to convict Ziggy Haskell, and nobody ever accused *him* of being a pansy.

Due to the lateness of the hour court was adjourned for the day. Victoria would have to wait until tomorrow to get a crack at Roberta Bristol.

CHAPTER THIRTY-EIGHT

When Victoria Edwards returned to her office she found me waiting for her. "Victoria, I need to speak with you—it's important."

"Of course, Ivy, please sit down."

"I have something to tell you that may have a bearing on the case. As you know, Bertrand Reynard was interning at my magazine. Mike Smythe's lady friend, Melinda, rents an office in our suite. I accidentally found out that Melinda and Bertrand were having a hot and heavy affair. When I heard Roberta Bristol's testimony that on the evening of the murder she saw Mike and Melinda going out, and then a little later she saw Bertrand enter Morgan House, I knew something was up. She thought that Mike had returned before then, but what if he hadn't? What was Bertrand doing going into Mike's house when he wasn't at home? How did he get in? Did he have a key? Did Mike leave the door unlocked? What if Mike came home while Bertrand was in his house doing whatever he was doing and caught him red-handed? What if Melinda knew about it? Bertrand has disappeared. Where? Why? Melinda says that she doesn't know where he is—is that the truth, or a lie?"

Victoria sat very still. I could see the wheels

turning. My cell phone rang. I saw that it was Detective Garrett calling. I wanted to speak with him privately, so I left Victoria's office. "John, have you found out anything about Tommy?"

"Not yet, but I followed your suggestion and checked out Charlotte, North Carolina. Turns out there was a terrible trucking accident there a few days ago. Several people were killed and there were a lot of injuries."

"Okay. Call me if there is any news." Detective Garrett could investigate Tommy's whereabouts, but I had a better source. I started for home to have a talk with Jaycee. Maybe if I tell her about the accidents in Charlotte she'll make a connection with Tommy. The snow was still coming down heavily, and the roads were very icy. I plowed my way from the Yukon to the front door and found Jaycee inside on her laptop, doing schoolwork, presumably. She was wearing her trademark gray sweatpants, and a giant tie-dyed T-shirt that brought back memories.

"Hi Mom, I'm surprised to see you home so early. I figured you'd probably stop by the office after court."

"Normally I would Jaycee, but something more important came up. Do you remember your dream about flying trucks?"

"Yes, Mom, sure I do."

"Do you remember telling me that Tommy

Monroe was in your dream, and that he called you Charlotte?

"Yes, I remember."

"Well, I spoke with Detective Garrett today, and he told me that Tommy Monroe went missing from Fort Hood several days ago." Jaycee gave me a puzzled look. "He has an idea that Tommy may have been involved in a trucking accident near Charlotte, North Carolina."

Jaycee sat back in her chair taking in the information. "Mom, what kind of the trucking accident was it?"

"I don't know, honey, Garrett didn't say. Let's see if we can find out on the Internet."

Jaycee started a Google search and soon we were looking at footage of the most bizarre site we'd ever seen. Huge gusts of wind blowing tractor-trailers right off the road and into the deep ravine below. We listened to a news report and learned that several people had died, and many were taken to local hospitals. Jaycee stared at the computer screen, but I could tell that she wasn't really looking at it. Her mind was off far away. Maybe she was having a psychic vision. I kept very quiet so as not to break the spell. After what seemed like an interminable length of time, Jaycee turned and looked at me and started talking rapidly. "Mom, I know where Tommy is. He's in a hospital in Charlotte. He's hurt pretty bad—all bandaged up. He doesn't remember who he is; he has amnesia. The hospital people don't know who he is; he didn't have any identification on him. Mom, we've got to help him."

Jaycee Googled hospitals in Charlotte, and made a list. I tried calling Garrett, but got no answer. There was no time to waste, so I decided to take matters into my own hands. Jaycee and I threw a few essentials in an overnight bag and headed for 79 South. The roads were bad; we made our way slowly but surely. The West Virginia mountains were going to be a bitch.

We finally arrived in Charlotte after a harrowing drive over the mountains. Jaycee had a long list of hospitals, and all I had to do was call every single one of them to find out if they had a young male patient with amnesia. Psychic visions could be tricky; they don't often give you the whole story. You just get the pieces, and then you have to figure it out like a puzzle. There was nothing else for us to do but get on with the search. After calling six hospitals without any luck, number seven showed promise. I struggled through an automated directory, and was finally able to reach a lady in admissions who remembered checking in a young man involved in the trucking accident. He was the only case she processed without identification, and to make matters worse the patient couldn't remember who he was when he came out of the coma. We headed for Charlotte General Hospital with the hope that he would find Tommy Monroe there.

The third-floor duty nurse showed us into room 306, a semi-private with a green curtain pulled shut between the two beds. I looked at the guy in the first bed. He was about seventy five years old—no go. On the other side of the curtain we hit the jackpot. It was Tommy all right; covered in bandages, but there was no mistaking his identity. He was awake, but one look into his eyes and I knew that he didn't have a clue who we were.

I made arrangements to talk to Tommy's doctors to see if he was well enough to leave the hospital. The doctors agreed that he was stable enough to go home, but as far as the amnesia went, only time would tell. I made arrangements for the discharge and we headed back to Pennsylvania. With luck, we'd be there by Monday morning. I called Garrett's cell. "I've got Tommy Monroe and we're on our way home."

"You *what?*"

I could hear the shock in his voice. "Jaycee and I found him in Charlotte. He's pretty banged up, and he's struggling with his memory, but I think he's coming out of it."

"Ivy, you took an awful chance going down there."

"The roads are still a nightmare. I'll call you when we reach Wellington," I said, anxious to end the call before he went into some kind of lecture.

I thought about John Garrett. Lately, he seemed

less anxious to minimize the possibility that Jaycee's psychic visions might actually have some value for shedding light on this case. I could kind of understand where his reluctance came from. Being a natural skeptic made him good at his job. Also, unless you had experience with psychics, it was really difficult to understand them. Most people thought that psychics see everything and can assess the situation immediately. That happens sometimes, but rarely. Mostly, the psychic will see bits and pieces of the picture, or get a partial message that has to be deciphered. Sometimes there is great detail, and other times the visions are vague. You just have to see how it plays out.

Having a psychic "gift" could be difficult to live with. There were times when it put a great strain on Jaycee. She struggled to understand much of what she saw, and it was often related to unpleasant circumstances, to say the least. She was also misunderstood by most people, and it caused her a great deal of pain at times. I really didn't envy her. There was one area in which I wished I had some psychic powers, or at least better insight. That was when it came to relationships. If only I had been better tuned into Bart—that is, the real Bart—I would've avoided intense heartache. His innate ability and well-honed skill at portraying a person he was not led me into an abyss of pain, confusion, and remorse that I found hard to shake.

After Bart's deceit and my foolish blind faith, how could I ever trust myself—how could I trust my judgment again? A man who appeared to be one thing on the surface, a loving husband and father, while leading a double life—and I didn't suspect a thing. But there was a lot more to it than that, feelings of my own inadequacies as a wife. What did Bart need that I didn't give him? What did he find in Marion that was lacking in me? Why did he feel that it was necessary to marry her, why not just have an affair? Maybe those were questions I would never be able to answer on my own.

CHAPTER THIRTY-NINE

Victoria Edward's opportunity to cross-examine Roberta Bristol had finally arrived. Roberta was in rare form. She was getting rather accustomed to testifying in court, and was actually becoming a star witness in the case. As such, she felt it best to look the part. She arrived in court wearing a striking purple suit accented with a large brimmed red felt hat that she purchased when she joined the "Red Hat Ladies Club." It was a statement declaring that women of a certain age were "still adventurous and capable of kicking up their heels!"

Victoria started right in. "Mrs. Bristol, you testified that the last time you saw Michael Smythe alive he was leaving his house with his lady friend."

"Yes, that's correct."

"Is she present in the courtroom today?"

Roberta looked directly at Melinda. "Yes, she is."

"Can you point her out for the court?"

Roberta aimed her finger straight at Melinda.

"Did you notice anything usual about them at the time?"

Melinda squirmed in her seat. Where was Victoria Edwards going with this? She could kill that Roberta Bristol.

Roberta was puzzled. "What do you mean unusual?"

"Well, for instance, were they wearing formal evening clothes? Were they carrying any bags or suitcases—that sort of thing."

"No, there was nothing unusual." Roberta thought back for a moment, "Wait, one thing that seemed unusual to me was that she drove. They got into her car and drove off. I've never seen that before. They always took his car, as far as I know."

Victoria considered this information. Why would Melinda drive on that particular evening? As far as she knew, there was nothing wrong with Smythe's car. Ivy saw it heading away from Morgan House when she arrived. That was after Smythe was dead. There could be several reasons, but Victoria had the feeling that Melinda drove that evening so that she could be in control of the leaving and returning. She could be in control of the whole evening. "Mrs. Bristol, you also testified that you saw Bertrand Reynard enter Morgan House that evening. Do you have any idea why he would be there?"

Ponzi was on his feet. "Objection, your Honor. Calls for conjecture on the part of the witness."

Lenny uttered "sustained."

Victoria knew that she had to get Roberta to make the connection between Bertrand and Melinda, but how? She decided to try a different tactic. "Mrs. Bristol, you mentioned that Bertrand Reynard was staying at your bed and breakfast. Why was he in Wellington?"

"Bertrand came over here from Paris; he's originally from Côte d' Ivoire, Africa." Roberta said this with pride, establishing the international ambiance of the Coach House B&B.

Victoria repeated her question. "Do you know what Bertrand Reynard was doing in Wellington?"

"He was here working on his doctoral dissertation. He was doing his internship with *Equine Style* magazine."

"Did he have any friends that you know of? Did anyone come to visit or call him?"

"No, he was kind of a loner, a fish out of water in Wellington. He did visit a lot with some guests from Algeria that stayed a while back, they all spoke French...and he spent a lot of time on Skype. I don't remember him having any visitors, and no one called Coach House to talk to him. He had his own cell phone. Oh, wait, I do remember that Mike Smythe's lady friend, that Melinda, called looking for Bertrand the morning after the murder. Of course, he was gone by then."

You could have heard a pin drop in that courtroom. Melinda sat frozen like a sculpture at the Ice Festival.

"Did she tell you why she was calling for Bertrand?"

"No, she's not one to divulge any information. She has an office in the *Equine Style* suite, but she doesn't work for them. She has something to do with the environment, so I doubt that she would be calling Bertrand on work-related matter."

"Objection, your Honor. Speculation on the part of the witness."

"Sustained." Lenny instructed Roberta to stick to the facts.

Victoria wanted to tie a neat little bow on this package. "Mrs. Bristol, according to your knowledge, Bertrand Reynard shared office space with Michael Smythe's lady friend at *Equine Style* and you received a call from this woman trying to reach Mr. Reynard at the Coach House on the morning after the murder. Is that so?"

"Yes. Those are the facts," Roberta said with emphasis on the word *facts*.

CHAPTER FORTY

Ponzi was getting a little worried. Victoria Edwards was diverting the jurors' attention away from Zachariah Haskell as the murderer and trying to pin it on someone else. He would have to work fast to establish Ziggy as the killer in the minds of the jury, or the kid might end up getting off. Ponzi couldn't afford a loss. He had ambitions in the D.A.'s office and he didn't want them to think he was losing his touch. Court was recessed for the weekend, so it would give him some time to rethink his strategy.

Ponzi wasn't the only one with worries. Melinda was about out of her skin. She thought she was going to have a nervous breakdown. She found herself getting closer and closer to the hot seat. The next thing you know Victoria Edwards would establish that she was the last person to see Mike Smythe alive, and they were tying her together with Bertrand. God, if they found out about his subversive activities it would be all over for her one way or another. Maybe it wasn't such a good idea to rat on him. Lord knows he deserved it, but now she might be left twisting in the wind alone. That bastard.

And what was with this D.A.? What an idiot. He was supposed to be building a case against Haskell, instead he was letting Edwards build a case against her. Well, that couldn't happen. She needed an alibi. She needed someone who would say that they saw her drop Mike Smythe off at his house and drive away. Who? Who would be stupid enough to stick their neck out like that? Melinda racked her brain; and then it came to her like a bolt of lightning—Biff Biddle. Good old ex-hubby Biff. He was the dumbest person she knew, and she was always able to manipulate him into doing whatever she wanted. She picked up the phone and punched in this number.

Biff answered on the third ring. When he heard Melinda's voice he was so stunned that he almost dropped the phone.

"Hello, Biffy, it's Melinda," she said in her sexiest voice.

"Melinda—oh wow, I'm surprised to be hearing from you." Surprised—shocked was more like it. Biff was amazed that he was able to even choke out those words.

"Surprised? I hope you're not disappointed," she said.

"Disappointed? Well, I just never thought you'd want to talk to me again, after the divorce and everything. Besides, didn't you go to New York and marry some guy there?"

"Oh Biff, that was over long ago. I'm back in Wellington now and I've been wanting to call you, but I was afraid you wouldn't want to hear from me."

"No, Melinda, I'm just surprised, that's all." Biff was lying through his teeth. He knew very well that Melinda was back. He even saw her in the courtroom, but he managed to avoid her—he didn't want any trouble.

"Biffy, the truth is that I need you. I have a bit of a problem, and you're the only man that I can turn to for help."

Biff was silent. He couldn't imagine what kind of problem Melinda could have that he would be able to fix.

"I don't want to talk about it on the phone. Could you please meet me at the Northwood for a drink? Say around six o'clock?"

"Okay, I suppose so," he said, knowing full well he was making a huge mistake.

"Thank you, Biffy—you're an angel. See you then."

Six o'clock rolled around in no time, and he found himself seated at a corner table in the bar at the Northwood Inn waiting for Melinda. He actually had been there for a while, and was working on his second beer. He needed some liquid courage for this meeting. At six o'clock, Melinda waltzed through the front door and surveyed the room looking for her prey. She was dressed in a tight black miniskirt, fishnet stockings, and red stilettos. It was a bit over-the-top, but this was an important mission. When she spotted Biff, she sauntered up to his table and stood stock-still waiting for his reaction.

"Hi, Melinda, you look great," he said as he pulled out a chair for her. That was an understatement. She looked hot. Her red low-cut blouse showed more than a hint of cleavage, and she was wearing his favorite perfume—*Poison.* Sex on a stick.

Melinda could see that she was getting the response she was looking for, so she dove right in. "Biffy, I'm so happy to see you. You're looking as virile as ever." She knew that she could risk being obvious—well, with Biff it wasn't a risk, it was a necessity. "Thank you so much for meeting me."

Curiosity was getting the better of him. "Melinda, you said that you are in some kind of trouble. What's wrong?"

"Oh, Biffy, it's about Mike Smythe's murder," she whined.

"What about it?"

"I think they're going to try and pin it on me."

"You?" Biff was shocked; he wasn't expecting this. "Why would they try that?"

"It looks like I might have been the last person to see Mike Smythe alive. We got together for cocktails on the evening of his murder. We were not together long, and afterward I dropped him off at his house and went directly home."

"Why don't you just tell them that Melinda?"

"Because I don't think that they would believe

me. And that Ivy Snow has been painting a pretty nasty picture of me."

Biff's mind flashed back to his last encounter with Ivy Snow. That bitch was a menace. "What can I do to help you, Melinda?"

Good, he was taking the bait. "Biffy, if you could just testify that you saw me drop Mike off at his house that night, and then drive away."

"What? I can't say that Melinda. That would be a lie. That would be perjury. I could go to jail!"

"Biffy, don't be silly. You're not going to go to jail. It's just a little white lie. Everyone tells little white lies." As the evening progressed, Melinda made a very convincing case to persuade Biff, especially later that night in her bedroom.

CHAPTER FORTY-ONE

Melinda stared at the plethora of clothes hanging in her closet. How she looked was always of the utmost importance, but never had it been so important as it was today. Today was the day she would be called to testify in court and the very thought of it made her nauseous. When it came to lying, her finely-honed skills had gotten her out of many "situations," but this was a whole new ballgame. She would be matching wits against lawyers that made their living wrangling the truth out of people, and she had to convince not only them, but also those twelve wild cards sitting in the jury box.

Knowing that she would find herself on the witness stand at some point, she made a careful study of the six men and six women who would be deciding the outcome of the case. This was a tough one. If it had been a jury made up of all men it would be a no-brainer. She would just wear a tight sweater and let her body language do the talking. But she would have to use more finesse if she were to gain credibility with the women. The foreman, and oldest of the six women, was a retired corporate executive with a stick up her ass. She would see right through Melinda's sex kitten act, and would resent her for the obvious attempt at manipulation. The woman had been wearing severely tailored suits every day since the trial began. She presented quite an authoritative persona. Melinda knew that her best bet with this woman would be to dress like her secretary probably had. Neat and efficient, but without sex appeal.

Two of the women jurors were housewives with children, who probably clipped coupons to make ends meet. A touch of polyester would be needed. Then there was a young "student activist" type, probably a member of NOW; a librarian, and a fitness trainer. The one characteristic that all of these women embodied was a "no-nonsense" attitude, so that would have to be the theme for Melinda's look. She chose a long-sleeved green polyester blouse (how did that even *get* in her closet?), a knee-length black bias cut skirt, and black leather ballerina flats. She decided to wear her hair pulled back in a silver barrette, and kept her makeup to a minimum. That should be perfect. Subtle, but convincing.

She gathered her things and headed toward her Mercedes. She realized that she was carrying her favorite Louis Vuitton handbag. That wouldn't do, so she exchanged it for a simple black leather tote, sans designer logos. She pulled her Mercedes into the garage three blocks from the courthouse. She didn't want any of jurors to see her driving an expensive car. She walked in the freezing cold, silently rehearsing her testimony. She had to convince the jury of three things. One, that she and

Mike Smythe were just casual friends. Two, that on the night of the murder she dropped Mike off at his house and went directly home. She would introduce the "fact" that she had waved to Biff Biddle as she pulled her car away from Mike's driveway, thus establishing her alibi. And three, that she had no idea who killed Smythe or why, and she barely knew Bertrand Reynard. She needed to distance herself from everyone in the case to establish her innocence.

Melinda was the first witness to take the oath that day. She felt slightly ill at ease taking the oath to tell the truth, the whole truth, and nothing but the truth, but she quickly shrugged it off. After all, truth is relevant. Ponzi approached the witness stand as Melinda made eye contact with Judge Lenny. Establishing rapport with the judge couldn't hurt. The prosecutor's first few questions were basic in nature—name, rank, and serial number. He wanted to get this over with as fast as he could, so that he could get down to the real business of getting Biddle to do an assassination number on Ziggy's character. He also needed to steer the jury away from the idea that this Melinda chick had anything to do with Smythe's murder. It was obvious that Victoria Edwards was heading in that direction, and he needed to squelch the idea before she convinced the jury of the possibility that Melinda was involved. Ponzi approached the witness stand and smiled at Melinda, hoping to put her at ease. "Were you acquainted with Michael Tellington Smythe?" he asked. He used the word *acquainted* to suggest a casual relationship.

"Yes," Melinda said.

How and when did you meet?"

"At a charity event at the Field & Stream Club a few years ago."

Ponzi nodded. He liked establishing the fact that they both supported charitable causes. "Had you seen Smythe often after that?"

Melinda paused before answering—this was tricky. "We saw each other at the club from time to time," she said. Technically, it wasn't a lie. It was true that they spent most of their time together at the Field & Stream Club, and as far as the frequency was concerned, it really depended on what one meant by *often*.

"When was the last time you saw Mr. Smythe?"

"It was on the night he died. I picked him up at his house, we had a drink at the Field & Stream Club, and I dropped him off at his house afterward. I then went directly home." Melinda stated the last part emphatically.

"Was there anyone who saw you drive away?"

"Yes. Just as Mike got out of the car and I pulled away from the curb, I saw Beaufort Biddle standing across the street. We waved to each other." Good. She had established her alibi.

"Thank you, that will be all; your witness,

counselor."

Victoria Edwards straightened her black pencil skirt and approached the stand. "You testified that you saw Michael Smythe from time to time. Could you please be more specific as to the nature of your relationship?"

You bitch, thought Melinda. "Michael Smythe and I were casual friends," she said.

Victoria raised her eyebrows. "Casual? Isn't it true that you dined with Smythe at the Field & Stream Club several times a week?"

"I didn't keep count," Melinda replied in a venomous tone.

"Would it surprise you if numerous employees at the club mentioned that they saw you having regular dates with Smythe, and that you exhibited amorous behavior that indicated that you were much more than just casual friends?"

"Yes. It would surprise me. Those people are not paid to gossip." Melinda regretted those words as soon as they came out of her mouth. She came off haughty and defensive. The last thing she wanted to do.

It was time for Victoria to put the pressure on. "Do you know a man by the name of Bertrand Reynard?"

Oh, my God, thought Melinda. What did they know about Bertrand and me? "Yes. He works in the same office building that I do."

"What is your relationship with Reynard?"

"We don't have a relationship. He just works in the same building. If you want to know about him, you should ask Ivy Snow. He works at her magazine."

"Do you know how Bertrand Reynard came to be employed at *Equine Style*?"

"No, certainly not." A bead of sweat began to break out on Melinda's forehead.

"Isn't it true you knew Mr. Reynard before he came to Wellington? That you met him in Paris last fall, and helped facilitate an internship at the magazine, which would be his ticket into the United States?"

Melinda just sat and stared at Victoria in shock. How did she know these things?

"Isn't it true that you had an affair with Reynard and agreed to help him obtain financing for a terrorist plot against the United States?" By now Victoria was practically shouting.

"That's insane!" Melinda screamed.

The courtroom was mesmerized. Ponzi sprang up from his chair. "Objection, your Honor. Counsel is badgering the witness."

"Overruled. The witness is instructed to answer the question."

By now Melinda was sweating profusely. "I don't know what you're talking about."

"Isn't it true that you and Reynard tried to blackmail Smythe, and when that didn't work, you arranged for Reynard to steal money that Smythe had hidden at Morgan House, while you kept him busy at the club?"

"No, no!" Melinda screamed. "I never blackmailed anybody. As a matter of fact, Smythe asked me for $100,000. I don't know if he was being blackmailed or not, he wouldn't tell me why he needed the money."

"Do you know why Smythe was being blackmailed?"

Roberta Bristol squirmed in her seat.

"I didn't say he was. I said he might have been. If Bertrand Reynard was blackmailing Smythe, I don't know why. I wasn't involved. I had nothing to do with stealing money from Mike Smythe. Bertrand Reynard is a liar and a criminal. You can ask him yourself if you can find him!"

Emotions in the courtroom were at a fevered pitch. Hardly the calm, orderly tone that Judge Lenny insisted on. He banged his gavel on the bench and called for order. Victoria didn't want to piss off the judge, so she decided to back off of Melinda—temporarily. "No more questions at this time, your Honor," she said. Court was recessed for lunch.

CHAPTER FORTY-TWO

Ponzi's head felt like it was being squeezed in a vise grip. He racked his brain for a way to convince the jury that Haskell was guilty. Now, thanks to Victoria Edwards, two other suspects, Bertrand and Melinda, were front and forward in the minds of the jury. He needed to change that—and fast. The little creep was guilty, of course, but proving it was another matter. No witnesses to the crime. No physical evidence to nail Haskell. Ponzi was going to have to go after a character assassination and maybe drag a confession out of the little bastard. He'd have to delve into Haskell's past and establish the kid as public enemy number one. He had a long way to go, but he had to start at the beginning. The kid had a rotten school record, so that was a good place to start.

As soon as court reconvened, Ponzi called Beaufort "Biff" Biddle, the Wellington High School guidance counselor, to the stand to try and establish the fact that Haskell was a rotten apple—always causing trouble and on the fast track leading to a life of crime.

Biff Biddle was nervous about testifying. He hated getting up on the stand in front of all those people, and that judge scared the hell out of him. Biff put his hand on the Bible and swore to tell the truth. Yeah, right, the truth according to Melinda. He spent hours, pretty good hours at that, he thought with a grin, crafting the story that he had seen her drop Mike Smythe off at his house on the night of the murder, and then drive off toward her house. It never happened, of course, but after hearing Melinda say it over and over it began to feel like it really did happen. Biff was hoping that maybe now that Smythe and Reynard were out of the way, he might get another chance with Melinda for good. He was making more money now—she'd be happy about that!

Ponzi strolled up to the witness stand holding his hands behind his back. "Mr. Biddle, are you acquainted with the defendant, Zachariah Haskell?"

"Yeah. I used to be his guidance counselor back when he was at Wellington High."

"Could you please tell the court about Zachariah's record while at school?"

"That kid was always getting into trouble. He got caught stealing stuff out of people's lockers. He was arrested for selling weed; he even set another kid's hair on fire once, but he did say that was an accident, and it probably was." Biff felt a little weird talking about all that stuff. Haskell wasn't the only kid doing shit like that back then.

Just then the doors at the back of the courtroom swung open and Ivy Snow walked in with a young guy covered in bandages. Biff recognized Tommy Monroe right away. He felt a lump harden in his throat.

"Mr. Biddle," Ponzi continued with his questions, and Biff further established the delinquent character of Zachariah Haskell.

"Your witness, Ms. Edwards."

Victoria's best bet here was to attack Biddle's credibility. Not an easy task with him being the esteemed guidance counselor that Ponzi made him out to be. "Mr. Biddle, while Zachariah Haskell was a student at your school, are you aware of any relationship between him and Michael Smythe?"

"What do you mean?"

"I mean, did it ever come to your attention that Haskell and Smythe knew each other, had an association of any kind?"

Biff thought back. He couldn't think of anything, but wait—the bus. "I think Haskell may have rode the school bus that Smythe drove from time to time." Biff looked at the back of the courtroom and saw Tommy Monroe staring at him. He loosened his tie.

Victoria saw her opening. "So Mr. Biddle, you're telling us that Smythe drove a Wellington school bus. Didn't you find that an odd occupation for a man of Michael Smythe's credentials?"

"Well, yeah, kinda."

"Why do you suppose that he chose such an unusual job?"

Ponzi objected again. "Calls for speculation on the part of the witness."

"Sustained."

Ponzi didn't like where this line of questioning was going. What was Victoria Edwards doing?

"Mr. Biddle, did Zachariah ever tell you anything about his relationship with Michael Smythe?"

Biff felt the heat rise up in his neck into his cheekbones.

"Mr. Biddle, please answer the question."

His tongue was so dry it stuck to the roof of his mouth. He struggled to speak, and managed to utter "no."

"Are you telling this court that you knew of no intimate relationship between Smythe and Haskell?"

"It wasn't exactly what you'd call a relationship. It was like this weird kind of situation between Smythe, Ziggy, and Tommy Monroe, Haskell's cousin," Biff blurted out.

The spectators buzzed. Lenny struck the bench with his gavel. "Order in the court."

Victoria turned up the heat. "Go on, Mr. Biddle, what about this situation, as you call it?"

Biff began to fall apart right there on the witness stand. It all came out in a rushing babble. "When he was fourteen, Tommy Monroe told me that Smythe got him and his cousin Ziggy drunk and raped them."

The courtroom went wild. Lenny banged his

gavel repeatedly. Tommy shot up from his seat and shouted, "I did it! I killed that son of a bitch! He ruined my life and he was gonna do the same thing to my little brother." A floodgate opened, and torrents of emotion poured out of Tommy's soul. Years of pent-up anger and shame were at last released. He buried his head in his hands and wept.

The courtroom was in chaos. Tommy's mother jumped up, screaming "no, no!" Ziggy's mother was in shock. Sandy Dobrowski sat very still, feeling intense cramps in her uterus. The bailiffs moved quickly, cuffing Tommy and pulling Ziggy away from the crowd.

Oh, my God—I looked over to see Sandy going into sudden labor. The cops had their hands full. I called 911 on my cell and sent for an ambulance. Ten hours later, Sandy delivered a healthy baby boy, Thomas Blaze Monroe II.

EPILOGUE

Thursday's Wellington Herald was chock-full of the Haskell murder trial's gory details. Anyone who wasn't present in the courtroom was "treated" to a blow-by-blow account of the proceedings, courtesy of Henry Melton, ace reporter. The story went that Michael Tellington Smythe, heir to a Pittsburgh steel fortune, was brutally murdered by Thomas Blaze Monroe in the living room of his own home, the historic Morgan House, in Wellington, Pennsylvania. Smythe had an illustrious career as the president of the Philadelphia Press, one of the country's most prestigious newspapers, and he was a well-respected conservative political adviser.

Smythe was home alone when he was visited by Tommy Monroe, a young soldier who had been born and raised in Wellington, and was absent without leave from Fort Hood, Texas. Monroe returned to Wellington with the intention of beating Smythe, who had allegedly said that he intended to have sex with Monroe's younger brother, Dale, age thirteen.

Monroe claimed that when he was fourteen years of age, Smythe raped him and his cousin Zachariah Haskell. Monroe stated that his intention was to "rough up" Michael Smythe in revenge and as a deterrent on his brother's behalf. The beating got out of hand, and Monroe bludgeoned Smythe to death with the pendulum from Smythe's own antique grandfather clock. In the meantime, Zachariah Haskell, who accompanied Monroe, entered Morgan House through the back door and set the kitchen curtains on fire. The men then stole Smythe's vintage Cadillac Eldorado to make their escape. Morgan House burned to the ground.

Investigation into the crime was led by Detective John Garrett of the Pennsylvania State police. Following a lead from the Wellington police, Garrett traced Haskell to Fort Hood, where the young private confessed to murdering Smythe. He was arrested and extradited to Pennsylvania. When Haskell learned that the cause of death was blunt force trauma to the head and not smoke inhalation, as he had previously believed, he changed his plea to not guilty.

District Attorney Paul Ponzi prosecuted Haskell, who was represented by public defender Victoria Edwards. In a surprise appearance on the fourth day of the trial, Private Thomas Monroe shocked the courtroom by confessing to Smythe's murder. Judge Leonard P. Clancy declared a mistrial.

Although Melton's account of this tragic event was technically correct, it lacked the nuance required to get the reader to the true heart of the story. The heinous crime of child rape was overshadowed by a crime of passion. What Melton failed to communicate was that Smythe's murder was the direct result of a chain of events that he himself set in motion many years ago. In reality, Smythe caused his own death, and took a collection of victims with him to the depths of hell.

The next few weeks were buried in the turmoil of acquitting Ziggy of Smythe's murder and charging Tommy with manslaughter. Ziggy was named an accessory, and was going to pay the price for arson. Melinda was convicted of perjury, and was sentenced to one-hundred seventy hours of community service picking up roadside trash. Beaufort Biddle was convicted of perjury and child endangerment, and was sentenced to three years in the state penitentiary. He was fired from his job in the Wellington School District, and lost his counseling license.

When I learned that Ziggy was responsible for the fire at Joe's, I was relieved. I wouldn't have to worry too much about Bart for a while. Sloane Parker had informed me that his request for parole had been denied. Ryan Adler was in the prison infirmary with a severe case of gout, so things would be quiet at Rockville—for the time being anyway.

Detective Garrett, John, called and asked me to join him for a drink at the Willow Inn.

"Ivy, I've got to say that this is the most bizarre case I've had in my twenty years on the force."

I shook my head and took a sip of my martini. "I can't help thinking that even though Smythe was the victim in this case, he was also the perpetrator. If it hadn't been for his sick, evil lifestyle none of this would have ever happened. There's such a thing as justifiable homicide, but there's no such thing as justifiable rape, especially of a child."

John put his hand over mine. "Ivy, I have to admit that without your help, and Jaycee's, we might have never gotten to the truth."

I smiled to myself. Wellington will never be the same—or will it?

ABOUT THE AUTHOR

Janet Winters fell in love with mysteries and horses thanks to Trixie Belden. After reading Trixie's first adventure, in which she and Honey cantered down the bridle path to solve a mystery, Janet was hooked. Then came Agatha, Sir Author, Rex, Daphne, and of course Dorothy L., who inspired her to name her horses after characters in the Lord Peter Wimsey series.

Janet was encouraged to write after winning a fifth-grade essay contest which was published in the local newspaper. After that, her writing took a deviant turn to ad copy, press releases, and commercials, for which she snagged a Matrix Award.

After thirty years of convincing people to buy things they didn't need, she turned to her real love— mysteries. She penned her first novel "Murder at Morgan House," introducing amateur sleuth Ivy Snow, her psychic teenage daughter Jaycee, and potential paramour Detective John Garrett. Together they expose deadly secrets that lie beneath the veneer of quintessential American small-town life.